Try to get proper ph from websites due You must be able - only

on her.

CW01429053

LAWRENCE:
A SILENT PASSING

A SCREENPLAY

MARK J.T. GRIFFIN

FIRST DRAFT
September 8, 2011

Notes
o Front Page Prelation?
• website.
o Box liner ??

Contacts
Gryffyn House
Wyre Lane
Long Marston
Stratford upon Avon
Warwickshire
CV37 8RQ
United Kingdom

Tel: +44 (0)1789 721875
Mob: +44(0)7885 530294

First Printed in 2011 in Great Britain
Copyright © 2011 by Mark J.T. Griffin

Published by
Mark J.T. Griffin
Gryffyn House
Wyre Lane
Long Marston
Stratford upon Avon
CV37 8RQ

ISBN 0-9533017-9-6 (First Edition)

To Ingrid with Love

By the Same Author

Biography
1994 **Vangelis: The Unknown Man**

Novels
1997 *going home*.
2006 *Richard of Eastwell*
2007 The Cathar Prophecy
2011 **ANGEL HOUSE**

Short Stories
2010 **Fairytales, Poems and Prophecies.**

Screenplays
2011 **Lawrence: A Silent Passing**

Contents

Synopsis

The story follows the last ten years of T.E. Lawrence's (Lawrence of Arabia), later T.E. Shaw's) life from 1925, the publication of "Seven Pillars of Wisdom", to his untimely and unexplained death in a motorcycle accident in 1935.

During that decade he centered his life at Cloud's Hill, his cottage near Bovington Camp in Dorset. During the period he built a strong circle of literary and artistic friends including Thomas Hardy (who lived close by), E.M. Forster, Siegfried Sasson, George Bernard Shaw, Henry Williamson and many others.

He also continued a friendship with Winston Churchill whom he had worked for during the Paris Conference, resolving the Arabian issues in the early 1920s. From this time onward Lawrence of Arabia spent the rest of his life escaping the epithet, using pseudonyms and changing his name. There is also strong evidence that, as for many other soldiers, he suffered from depression bought on by Post-War Syndrome.

His uncompromising and direct manner had created many enemies. In 1927, to get him "out of the way" he was posted for a short while to Karachi, at that time part of India. Returning to England he began designing RAF speedboats for search and rescue and helped to push a Bill through Parliament to abolish the death penalty for cowardice.

Early in 1935, the year of his death, Churchill began discussing with him a new role in preparation for what Churchill believed was war with Germany. The role would have had Lawrence replace Major-General Waldegrave Kell as the Head of the Secret Service – both MI5 and MI6.

At 11.30am, May 13 1935, 46-year-old Lawrence was riding his motorcycle along a straight stretch of road between Bovington Camp and his cottage at Clouds Hill. At the same time, two teenage boys were cycling pedal bikes in the same direction.

For some reason, Lawrence suddenly collided with the back wheel of one of the boy's bikes and was thrown off his motorcycle, fracturing his skull. He never regained consciousness and died six days later.

past or passing

At the inquest, eyewitness Corporal Ernest Catchpole said he had seen a black car traveling at speed pass Lawrence in the opposite direction just before the crash. The circumstances of his death continue to be a mystery and there is strong evidence that with a *potential position being built for him by Churchill* within the Secret Service in preparation of World War II, his death was a conspiracy engineered by MI5.

The screenplay is a historically accurate British period drama. A character study of a man many regarded as a hero for the 20th century. It uses extracts from letters and other contemporaneous documents to reconstruct Lawrence's life, the accident, the inquest and Lawrence's funeral and explores why there was a conspiracy to have him murdered.

(may have been)

Chronologically the story follows on from David Lean's "Lawrence of Arabia" (1962) with Peter O'Toole playing Lawrence and "Dangerous Man: Lawrence After Arabia" (1992) with Ralph Fiennes in the title role.

* *with Churchill creating a potential ...*

? *of* ?

Do a 'Find & Replace' on Cloud's to Clouds Hill! It's all through the book

Author's Note: Images are included within the screenplay to give the reader an insight in the man, the characters and the locations.

of

Dramatis Personae

Lead Characters

T.E. Lawrence also known as T.E. Shaw	Also know as Lawrence of Arabia. Lawrence changed his name officially in 1927 from T.E. Lawrence to T.E. Shaw. For clarity he is always referred to as Lawrence though his friends and family knew him as Ned. He would have been 35 in 1924. See Biographies section.
Corporal Ernest Catchpole	Later Sergeant. Witness to the T.E. Lawrence accident
Albert Hargraves	Boy; Aged 14. Butcher's Boy. Bicyclist involved and injured in the accident.
Frank Fletcher	Boy; Aged 14. Friend of Albert Hargraves. Second bicyclist involved in the accident.
Thomas Hardy	Author and Writer (Tess of the D'Urbervilles, Mayor of Casterbridge, Jude the Obscure etc) He is 84 when he first enters the screenplay. See Biographies section.
Florence Hardy	Thomas Hardy's wife; 39 years Hardy's junior – would have been 45 in 1925.
E.M. Forster	Author and Writer (Passage to India, Room with a View etc). Aged 46 in 1925.
Sydney Smith	Friend and colleague of T.E.'s. His CO on his return from India. His wife Clare exchanged letters with TE.
Arthur Russell	Army friend of T.E.'s
E "Posh" Palmer	Army friend of T.E.'s
Sharif Ali	His brother in arms in Arabia. Note: played by Omar Sharif in "Lawrence of Arabia".
Major Ralph Neville-Jones	Coroner at the Inquest for T.E. Lawrence.

Lead Characters (Continued)

Winston Churchill	Conservative Leader, Politician, War-time Prime Minister. A friend of T.E. Lawrence from 1920 when Lawrence was an advisor. See Biographies .
Major-General Sir Vernon Kell.	Head of British Secret Service - MI5 (also known as "K").
John Handler	An MI5 thug. His sophisticated exterior disguises his violent and ruthless approach. Fictitious.
Peter Page	A journalist for Beaverbrook newspapers and an MI5 operative. He is driven by alcohol and financial rewards rather than by doctrine.
John Prentice	A junior officer in the Royal Army Ordinance Corp (RAOC).
Douglas "Monty" Cake	His friend; another officer in the army (RAOC) .
Captain Charles Allen	Captain Charles Allen of the Royal Army Medical Corp.
Captain Hyde-Pierce	Corporal Catchpole's officer in command. Fictitious.
George Brough	Motorcycle manufacturer, known for his powerful Brough Superior motorcycles which were the first super bikes. Aged 45 at the time of Lawrence's death.
MP Sergeant	Military Police Sergeant
Post Master	Post Master of Bovington Post Office .
Lord Lloyd	Conservative politician; formerly High Commissioner to Egypt; friend of TE, mourner at his funeral.
Lady Nancy Astor	Politician, friend and mourner at T.E.'s funeral .
Gin the dog	Prentice's Sealyham bitch.
Wessex the dog	Hardy's long-haired terrier.

Leads – Voice Only

Viscount Allenby	T.E. Lawrence's CO during his time in Arabia. ~~Voice only~~.
BBC Newsreader	Has an "Alvar Liddel" BBC voice. ~~Voice only~~.
Henry Williamson	Author and Writer (Tarka the Otter, etc); involved in the English Fascist Movement. Aged 30 in 1925.

Minor Leads

Driver	RAF Driver at Cattewater
Nurse	Nurse in Bovington Hospital Intensive Care
Reporter	Reporter T.E. assaults at Clouds Hill
Photographer	Photographer T.E. assaults at Clouds Hill
Police Sergeant	Police officer bribed by Peter Page
Pat Knowles	Pall bearer at T.E.'s funeral. Friend, neighbour of T.E.
Col. Newcombe	Pall bearer at T.E.'s funeral. Friend and colleague of T.E.
Sir Ronald Storrs	Pall bearer at T.E.'s funeral. Friend and colleague of T.E.
Aircraftman W. Bradbury	Pall bearer at T.E.'s funeral. Friend of T.E.
Eric Kennington	Pall bearer at T.E.'s funeral. Friend of T.E.; will make T.E.'s effigy in St Martin's Church, Wareham

Extras

Jury	Jury at the inquest. Twelve "local" men; half of which are soldiers.
Congregation	Congregation of St Nicholas' Church Moreton for T.E.'s funeral
Soldiers	Witnesses to the accident

Full stops behind every sentence in r/h section of tables!

Scene 1 – Opening Credits			
Location	Opening Credits	**Est. Run Time**	02:00

Synopsis
Opening Credits, Introduction to T.E. Lawrence's past in Arabia, his poetic character and a feeling of peace after the turmoil of war.

BEGIN OPENING CREDITS AND TITLES

TITLES (suggest black with burnt red letters)

Lawrence: a Silent Passing / لورانس : أ تمرير الصامت :

Crescent **Dissolve to:**

Exterior / SKY, CRESENT MOON, STARS   Night

Dissolve to:

Exterior / BLUE SKY   Day

A beautiful blue sky on an English summer day. The sounds of gently rustling trees and skylarks fill the air.

CAPTION: *All men dream, but not equally. Those who dream by night in the dusty recesses of their minds, wake in the day to find that it was vanity: but the dreamers of the day are dangerous men, for they may act on their dreams with open eyes, to make them possible. This I did.*

SOUND of motorbike approaching and fading into the distance.

CAMERA PANS towards the brightness of a hot sun echoing the desert heat.

END OPENING CREDITS AND TITLES

Scene 2 – Accident			
Location	Bovington Camp Road, Dorset	**Est. Run Time**	03:30

Synopsis
The scene shows the suspicious circumstances of T.E.'s motorcycle accident. It includes the black car, witnesses and the two delivery boys on bicycles with whom he collides.

Cut to:

Exterior / BLUE SKY   Day

> T.E. LAWRENCE V/O
> *I loved you, so I drew these tides of men into my hands and wrote my will across the sky in stars.*

CAMERA PANS from sun and sky to a deserted country lane lined with gorse bushes and pine trees; typical Dorset heath land. The long strip of black road stretches off in a straight line to the horizon. The road, though straight, has a few dips in it.

CAPTION: 13th May 1935. Bovington, Dorset

Cut to:

Exterior / BOVINGTON LANE, DORSET   Day

On a quiet country lane two boys on old black delivery bicycles come into view. They are pedaling slowly and enjoying the day, weaving a little on the empty road.

> FRANK FLETCHER
> *Come on Albert! Keep up! We're never going to get to Moreton Woods at this rate!*

ALBERT HARGRAVES
All right Frank; I'm pedaling fast as a can! This
bike weighs a ton!

FRANK FLETCHER
Anymore deliveries?

ALBERT HARGRAVES
Nah. That's it for today. We should still have
plenty of time for collecting nests.

Behind ALBERT and FRANK is the distant sound of a motorbike coming towards them at speed. The boys continue to pedal and are almost side by side. FRANK is slightly in front. They are chatting and are more concerned with their plans than the road. Unconsciously they move to single file with FRANK in front of ALBERT. Unseen by them coming towards them is a black car. A 1934 Wolsely 21/60. The boys do not notice it and are pre-occupied.

A few hundred yards ahead of the boys on the right hand side of the lane is a cluster of 20 army tents camped on the heath. The camp is a hive of activity with cooking fires, game of cricket, soldiers lazing in the sun.

Cut to:

Exterior / BOVINGTON LANE, CAMP FENCE   Day

On the edge of the camp walking along the low boundary fence of the camp looking towards the road is a soldier smoking a cigarette. It is CORPORAL ERNEST CATCHPOLE.

Above the sound of the car CATCHPOLE can also hear the sound of the motorbike coming towards him.

SLOW MOTION. The black car passes him at speed traveling at approximately 60 miles per hour. It is almost driving in the centre of the road.

CATCHPOLE very briefly sees the driver and the passenger in the back seat on the driver's side. They look suspicious; intense. They are both dressed smartly, wearing trilby hats, pinstriped suits and ties.

EXTREME SLOW MOTION. As the car passes ahead of him, now level with the boys CATCHPOLE sees the car door open slightly. It is something he can't explain. It is just not right.

The car disappears into the dip in the road.

Cut to:

Exterior / BLUE SKY   Day

A beat of a second. All is peace and calm.

Cut to:

Exterior / BOVINGTON LANE   Day

A black Brough Superior SS100 motorcycle GW 2275 appears from the dip in the road coming towards the boys and CATCHPOLE.

The motorcycle is ridden by T.E. LAWRENCE who is wearing goggles, blue overalls but no helmet. The bike is seriously out of control weaving all over the road.

POV T.E. LAWRENCE face-on we see the eyes of T.E. LAWRENCE; they are wide, there is fear in them.

The motorbike careers into ALBERT'S bike who, in turn, is pushed into the back wheel of FRANK'S bike.

CORPORAL CATCHPOLE throws away his cigarette and runs towards the accident.

ALBERT falls from his bike and is thrown a few yards from his bike. He is still. A few coins - coppers from his pocket - tumble into the tarmac tinkling on the ground.

FRANK falls from his bike but after dusting himself off gets up almost immediately.

T.E. LAWRENCE is thrown over the handle bars of the motorbike and he slides down the road with huge force. The momentum carries him and the bike down the road. The bike ends up behind him. His head hits the tree and he ends up against the tree, propped up against it in a sitting position.

FRANK runs past ALBERT who is moving his legs (he is still alive at least) and over to where T.E. LAWRENCE is against the tree. He arrives a moment before CATCHPOLE and they stand before T.E. LAWRENCE.

Other soldiers from the camp begin to run up the road and towards the accident scene.

Through a strange desert-like haze T.E. LAWRENCE can see the boy (FRANK) with the sun behind him. He imagines it is an Arab boy that he knows.

His eyes begin to glaze over. His head is gradually being covered with blood from his crown to his neck until only his intense blue eyes are visible.

His eyes now stare fixed towards the cloudless blue sky.

> T.E. LAWRENCE (whispering)
> *Dahoum?*

His eyes mist over, his lids flutter and close and he is still.

Scene 3 – Cloud's Hill Party

Location	Clouds Hill Cottage	Est. Run Time	07:30

Synopsis
The scene introduces Lawrence and his home, his relationships with famous writers of the time. It shows his depressive nature and volatile character.

space

Cut to:

NEWSREEL LAWRENCE'S time in Arabia, Paris Conference and return to England.

Cut to:

Interior / CLOUD'S HILL COTTAGE, DORSET   Day

CAPTION: Eleven Years Before. 21st June 1924.

CAMERA PANS up the narrow staircase into an upstairs study/sitting room in the cottage seemingly filled with people chatting and talking. A social scene.

A fire crackles briskly in the hearth. On the mantelpiece, grate and strategically placed around the room candles burn giving more light. The room has a large leather sofa and in the corner a large white horn for an ECM gramophone which is playing a piece of Beethoven which bathes the room with music.

MUSIC: Beethoven Symphony No. 6 in F - Allegro

Five people are seated in the room. They are THOMAS HARDY, FLORENCE HARDY, E.M. FORSTER and two soldiers in army green but "at ease". The soldiers are PRIVATE ARTHUR RUSSELL and PRIVATE E "POSH" PALMER. WESSEX THE DOG – Hardy's long-haired terrier sleeps by FLORENCE'S feet.

E.M. FORSTER
A primitive little house but curiously welcoming! But thank heavens for the fire!

ARTHUR RUSSELL
Bitter cold in the winter but Ned's making considerable improvements.

T.E. LAWRENCE is standing in the doorway with a tray of mugs that steam with freshly-brewed tea. He is quite a short man but well-built for that. He is dressed in army green with his shirt collar open.

T.E. LAWRENCE
..And it's colder than a desert winter even in the summer.

He hands out the tea to his guests who smile at the rough mugs they are given. He gives WESSEX a biscuit.

T.E. LAWRENCE
My friends I propose a toast. To the "Seven Pillars of Wisdom"!

ALL (a toast)
"The Seven Pillars of Wisdom"!

POSH PALMER
And God Bless all who sail in her!

ARTHUR RUSSELL
Liable to sink if they do!

THOMAS HARDY
Oh, I think not! I'm a proud subscriber and it's an impressive undertaking.

ARTHUR RUSSELL
It is to be sure – but the title?

T.E. LAWRENCE
Book of Proverbs Chapter 9 Verse 1: "Wisdom hath built her house, she hath hewn out her seven pillars".

He smiles, a memory rises to the surface.

T.E. LAWRENCE (Continuing)
I knew it as a splendid rock formation near Wadi Rum. We based our operations there in 1917.

POSH PALMER
And when is it due in print?

T.E. LAWRENCE
Hopefully by Christmas – other subscribers permitting.

POSH PALMER
And with many other erudite friends you will have no problem at all.

T.E. LAWRENCE
I'm surprised anyone would want to read it.

E.M. FORSTER   *past*
There are a great many Lawrence; that terrible war is only six years passed and fresh in the minds of the people. They still question how it happened. They seek answers.

THOMAS HARDY
God forbid it is ever as dark again.

T.E. LAWRENCE (bitterly)
That is the stupidity of man. Short memories and long knives. Sadly we cannot guarantee it won't happen again. And the insanity of those pompous asses in command.

Looks to RUSSELL and PALMER

Page 16 of 120

> T.E. LAWRENCE (continuing)
> *We see it every day.*

Russell and Palmer nod in agreement.

> T.E. LAWRENCE (continuing, bitterly)
> *The same insanity that got tens of thousands slaughtered, sons, brothers, fathers, husbands and friends lost.*

He glances over to the picture of his friend Dahoum on the mantelpiece.

> T.E. LAWRENCE (continuing)
> *A lost generation. They sent them to the slaughter like cattle in an abattoir. To me an unnecessary action, or shot, or casualty, is not only waste but sin.*

LAWRENCE hits the mantelpiece with his fist in frustration. The social atmosphere is broken by an awkward silence. Consciences are pricked.

> T.E. LAWRENCE (continuing, calmly)
> *Yes. Many friends lost.*

He runs his hands gently on the edge of the photo frame. Florence Hardy breaks the stony silence.

> FLORENCE HARDY
> *Do you yearn for those days and nights in the desert?*

LAWRENCE closes his eyes; in his mind he is transported. He can hear the sound of fighting, shots, screams of the dying. A tumultuous battle rages in his head.

SOUND FX: DESERT BATTLE, SCREAMS, SHOTS.

> FLORENCE HARDY
> *Ned? Ned?*

Raises her voice to attract his attention.

> *Ned!*

LAWRENCE wakes from his dream and shakes the mood away.

> T.E. LAWRENCE
> *Sorry. Yes. And No.*

LAWRENCE examines the grass plant on the mantelpiece – a souvenir from Aqaba. PALMER tries to lighten the atmosphere.

> POSH PALMER (to Russell)
> *As enigmatic as ever; always battling one demon or another!*

> T.E. LAWRENCE
> *The truth? It was a brutal and violent time but a necessary one. It was a different time that needs must I will try to forget. Truly the best of times and the worst of times.*

> E.M. FORSTER
> *Dickens! Forget yes, we all try. But will you try to forgive?*

> T.E. LAWRENCE
> *OU ØPOVTIS.*

In Greek and pronounced "oo frontis"; translated in English as "who cares?" or "why worry".

> E.M. FORSTER
> *Herodotus! And of course we all care Ned!*

FORSTER looks around to the others and receives their support and agreement.

> E.M. FORSTER (continuing)
> *By the way why didn't you just put "welcome" over your door?*

T.E. LAWRENCE
Because there are many that are not welcome and very few who really do care.

FLORENCE HARDY
Do the higher echelons still bother you?

T.E. LAWRENCE
Always. One new project or another. I know they really just tolerate me - I'm not sure they know what to do with me. I still hold some sway though. Winston is still a good friend.

THOMAS HARDY
Churchill?

T.E. LAWRENCE
Yes. Helps when he can; warns me of any trouble brewing.

FLORENCE HARDY
Trouble?

T.E. LAWRENCE
The honourable gentlemen of the press. Bloody jackals! One day they will be the death of someone, mark my words. Mind you I always invent a story for them to print. Pack of lies of course but keeps me amused!

FLORENCE HARDY
And the Seven Pillars – your book? How many sponsors do you have?

T.E. LAWRENCE

G.B.

GB Shaw's agreed, Siegfried, my chums here. X
Buchan. They've all stumped up their 15 guineas. No real people of course?

E.M. FORSTER
Who are the real people?

Page 19 of 120

ARTHUR RUSSELL
Ned insists that he should avoid real people at all costs. Say's that the army is gradually dyeing him khaki.

POSH PALMER
Does it to all of us! Rots you from the outside from flesh pink to rotting green.

ARTHUR RUSSELL
Bloody well right Ned!

T.E. LAWRENCE (an announcement)
I've asked to be transferred. To the RAF.

ARTHUR and POSH look at each other. This is news to them. They seem surprised, perhaps betrayed.

ARTHUR RUSSELL
What? Why Ned?

POSH PALMER
When? For what reason?

T.E. LAWRENCE
I expect shortly. To be sure the days and nights with my colleagues and the company are incomparable. The minutes and hours however, are simply unbearable.

ARTHUR RUSSELL
You think you can swing it?

T.E. LAWRENCE
Interesting turn of phrase. If I can't there's plenty a beam that will bear my "littlest" weight.

ADLIB: Sighs and exasperation from the guests.

E.M. FORSTER
Come now Ned! A rather over-dramatic gesture?

T.E. LAWRENCE
When life becomes unbearable for the soul, the soul is all the more eager to depart it.

POSH PALMER
You have everything to live for. Not least for your friends.

Font size'

ARTHUR RUSSELL
Agreed you miserable blighter.

RUSSELL looks at the rough mug disparagingly.

ARTHUR RUSSELL (continuing)
Where the hell did you get these?

T.E. LAWRENCE (lightly)
Threw them myself. No I did! Over at the Sandford pottery just outside Wareham.

ARTHUR RUSSELL
Then if the RAF won't have you, you still have a burgeoning career as a potter ahead of you!

FORSTER has risen from his chair to examine a book on the mantelpiece

E.M. FORSTER
George Bernard Shaw. Saint Joan of Arc. You have his new work I see.

T.E. LAWRENCE
G.B.
Yes. GB and Charlotte are close friends. He has signed it.

E.M. FORSTER (Opens the book)
From Private Shaw to Public Shaw!

ADLIB: General amused laughter from the guests.

> T.E. LAWRENCE
> *GB has wicked sense of humour eh?*

> ARTHUR RUSSELL
> *Have you read it yet?*

> T.E. LAWRENCE
> *Of course; the day it arrived in the post. A little verbose in places but…*

> E.M. FORSTER
> *My God; you are a literary critic!*

FORSTER passes the book to RUSSELL.

> T.E. LAWRENCE
> *Honest rather than critical.*

> ARTHUR RUSSELL
> *May I?*

RUSSELL indicates he would like to borrow it.

> T.E. LAWRENCE
> *Of course! But for God's sake give it back.*

> THOMAS HARDY
> *Tread carefully Forster. He does not save his censure even for me!*
> T.E. LAWRENCE
> *Now Thomas, surely not censure. You write a good tale but too descriptive. You need to get to the meat of the story. Do you not agree that the first draft is all – all the revision will not save a first bad draft?*

> THOMAS HARDY
> *To be sure. If it flows like the River Frome then it will find its way to a sea of readers.*

T.E. LAWRENCE

God knows how many ornamentations Seven Pillars went through. I had the first draft manuscript stolen on the train once. Had to start all over again!

THOMAS HARDY

Surely it's just a question of taste and palate?

T.E. LAWRENCE

Agreed, but I like to skip the hors d'oevres and get onto the main course.

E.M. FORSTER

You'd agree, to build a strong house you need firm and robust foundations?

T.E. LAWRENCE

Yes but even tents may have a view of the stars!

ADLIB Laughter from the guests and the party continues.

FADE TO NEXT SCENE.

Scene 4 – Friendship with Florence			
Location	Clouds Hill Cottage	**Est. Run Time**	02:00

Synopsis

The scene shows Lawrence's friendship with Florence Hardy, his continued thoughts of his time in Arabia and a man wrestling with demons and darkness.

Space   **Fade to:**

Exterior / CLOUD'S HILL GARDEN   Day

CAMERA PANS across a sandy heather bank of flowering purple rhododendron bushes. Arthur Russell, Posh Palmer and E.M. Forster are climbing the bank further onto the heath to explore. HARDY stands with WESSEX in a corner of the garden enjoying the view.

CAMERA PANS onto FLORENCE HARDY and LAWRENCE sitting on chairs in the sunshine, they are listening to the wind in the trees, birds, skylarks. LAWRENCE hears a rustling in the bushes and Wessex appears from the bush. LAWRENCE opens his eyes, startled.

> FLORENCE HARDY (not opening her eyes)
> *Never really relax do you Ned?*

> T.E. LAWRENCE
> *A Bedouin affectation I'm afraid.*

> FLORENCE HARDY
> *Are you well Ned? You seem, a little depressed. I mean after that nonsense about suicide.*

> T.E. LAWRENCE (bitterly)

Page 24 of 120

Consequence of a war. Days and nights of brutality.

FLORENCE HARDY
Do you miss it? The desert I mean. Your comrades?

T.E. LAWRENCE
The desert is a place without nuance; only light and dark. This world blurs distinctions. The desert? I never really left; my heart lies there still.

FLORENCE HARDY
Not surprising – you were a hero then. Now...

T.E. LAWRENCE (modestly)
Now? Plain Private Shaw. If I change the name the myth that was Lawrence of Arabia can be buried. Besides the hero epithet is overused. I've been and am absurdly over-estimated. There are no supermen and I'm quite ordinary.

FLORENCE HARDY (doubting him)
But surely Ned...

T.E. LAWRENCE
In that point I'm one of the few people who tell the truth about myself.

FLORENCE HARDY
Modesty Ned. Your gallantry in the desert? Giving back what was theirs.

LAWRENCE gazes across an English garden in full bloom. Wessex is running around enjoying the freedom of space.

T.E. LAWRENCE

Page 25 of 120

Men have looked upon the desert as barren land, the free holding of whoever chose. In fact each hill and valley in it had a man who was its acknowledged owner and would quickly assert the right of his family or clan to it, against aggression.

FLORENCE HARDY
And in making this gift you made many friends.

T.E. LAWRENCE
And enemies. Many enemies. But my friends, my brothers in blood and arms. I loved and will never be loved again.

FLORENCE looks towards Russell, Palmer and Forster who are helping Thomas Hardy walk down some garden steps.

FLORENCE HARDY
But surely....

T.E. LAWRENCE
People aren't friends till they have said all they can say, and are able to sit together, at work or rest, hour-long without speaking. We never got quite to that, but were nearer it daily. Since he died I haven't experienced any risk of that happening. So. No. Never again. Dahoum was my friend and companion. He was simple. Without...

He searches for the right word.

T.E. LAWRENCE (continuing)
...baggage.

FLORENCE HARDY
One day you will find peace again I'm sure.

Page 26 of 120

T.E. LAWRENCE
I'm not so sure Florence. All those battles. Damascus, Medina, Aqaba, Tafas, Derra – they have all left their scars on me. Even when the world is at peace I seem not to be. My blood flows down different paths (than) other men. And all I see is insanity, cruelty, I cannot rest.

FLORENCE HARDY
Keep searching for your peace Ned.

FLORENCE touches his hand in comfort.

FLORENCE HARDY (continuing)
Seek. And you will find.

Scene 5 – Friends Depart

Location	Clouds Hill Cottage	Est. Run Time	02:30

Synopsis
The scene shows Lawrence's
friends departing from the party.

Cut to:

Exterior / CLOUD'S HILL COTTAGE GARDEN   Day

It is almost sunset, the party is breaking up. Hand shakes, hugs and kisses are exchanged. RUSSELL shakes hands with Lawrence, looks at his watch and then turns to Posh Palmer.

> ARTHUR RUSSELL
> *Come on Posh! We'd better pedal back to the camp. See you at parade Ned.*

They both rush away.

> T.E. LAWRENCE (sarcastically)
> *Just you try keeping me away!*

> FLORENCE HARDY (to LAWRENCE)
> *Now, you must come over to Max Gate next week. We have the "Curse of the House of Arenas" being played on the back lawn. Thomas has invited the "The Balliol Players".*

> T.E. LAWRENCE
> *Ah! Old Oxfordians.*

LAWRENCE and FLORENCE exchange kisses on the cheek.

Page 28 of 120

T.E. LAWRENCE (continuing)
Perhaps, but I may have to….

FLORENCE HARDY
Now none of your excuses. Thomas and Forster will be there and it's not a party without you no matter what you think of yourself.

T.E. LAWRENCE
Quite so. I may bring Arthur and Posh as well, if you don't mind having them foisted on you again.

FLORENCE HARDY
Not at all; I also wanted to talk to you about editing Thomas' memoirs.

THOMAS HARDY
Oh not those raw ramblings again.

T.E. LAWRENCE (smiling). submeshed?)
It would be a pleasure and an honour Florence.

As voices disappear down the lane LAWRENCE sighs and looks up the garden.

CAMERA follows LAWRENCE as he walks to his garage and opens the garage door.

Sitting in the middle of the garage is a gleaming Brough Superior SS100 motorbike. He picks up a rag and polishes the bike with obvious love and care.

T.E. LAWRENCE
Ah Boanerges. You are the silkiest thing. Truly the Son of Thunder.

Scene 6 – A New Posting

Location	Clouds Hill Cottage	Est. Run Time	00:30

Synopsis
Lawrence receives the bad news of his RAF posting to India.

Cut to:

Exterior / CLOUD'S HILL GARDEN   **Day**

CAPTION: 13th September 1926

It is a miserable grey day, it is raining torrentially and thunder rumbles in the distance.

CAMERA PANS from tree level down through the rain to LAWRENCE standing in the doorway of the cottage.

In his left hand he holds a brown envelope and in the right a letter which he is reading.

> T.E. LAWRENCE V/O
> *...this is to confirm your posting to RAF Depot, Drigh Road, Karachi, India. You will be assigned to the Engine Repair Section as a clerk. Your posting will commence from....*

He scrunches the envelope and idly drops the letter where it lands in a puddle of water. The rain dissolves the ink on the paper. LAWRENCE turns his back on the rain and walks back into cottage.

Fade to next scene.

Scene 7 – Letter from India – 1

Location	RAF Depot, Karachi, India	Est. Run Time	01:30

Synopsis

Lawrence has been posted to India. He is bored and home-sick and spends most of his free time writing to friends in England.

Cut to:

Exterior / RAF DEPOT, KARACHI, BARRACKS   Day

CAPTION: May 1927, RAF Depot, Karachi   *Contrast wk vs India*

The door to the office is open on a dusty and hot day. The breeze blows the net curtains from the doors. From behind the camera we can hear the occasional sounds of a car, a plane engine, and soldiers at drill.

Lawrence sits in the doorway of the barracks writing a letter and occasionally ~~smiling~~ *smiles* as he writes.

He rocks on the chair~~, occasionally~~ *&* rises as he reads back his writing.

> T.E. LAWRENCE V/O
> *Karachi. 5th May 1927. Dear Mrs Hardy, I should have answered your letter three months back, but you know how it is, especially in this place, which is just a hot-storage for me, for the years which must pass before I may return to England. Somehow letter-writing rubs in the sense of being away.*

T.E. LAWRENCE V/O (continuing)
Charlotte Shaw kindly sent me a gramophone which helps to break the monotony and she tells me G.B. wishes to use my character in a future play. He names the character Private Napoleon Meek! Is it any wonder I have changed my name to honour my friend and hero! I am now officially T.E. Shaw. Perhaps this will somehow begin to erase the trail of Lawrence?

FLASHBACK: WESSEX the dog is running around Cloud's Hill garden playing.

TE LAWRENCE V/O (continuing)
The death of Wessex the dog is a loss to me. He was so firm and decisive a being, one who always knew his own mind, and never hesitated to change it, if he thought fit. So doing he showed a very healthy disregard of the feelings of merely temporary visitors. Few dogs appeal to me, but Wessex gained my very definite respect. Max Gate will not seem quite right now. He must be a very great loss to you and T.H. I'm so sorry.

Cut to:

Exterior / RAF DEPOT, KARACHI, BARRACKS   Day

T.E. LAWRENCE (Continuing)
I hope you and T.H. are otherwise well. I'm grateful for your kindly judgement of "The Seven Pillar's. It is inevitable that people should call it less good than the 'Oxford' text, but their judgement leaves me cold. Only I have read the two so closely as really to see the differences: and my taste in every case approved the changes.

LAWRENCE takes an apple from his pocket and takes a bite from it.

Page 32 of 120

T. E.

TE LAWRENCE V/O (continuing)
The Cape abridgement is selling like ripe apples, they tell me. I hate that little book.

My restlessness, on first seeing Karachi, has faded. I keep myself strictly to camp, and make my time pass easily enough with books, reading and re-reading the old things I have read and liked, but not treated ceremoniously enough, in my youth. Yours ever, T E Shaw.

Fade to next scene.

T. E

Scene 8 – Letter from India – 2			
Location	RAF Depot, Karachi, India	**Est. Run Time**	03:00

Synopsis	
Lawrence writes to Florence Hardy. He has heard that Thomas Hardy has died and writes a grief-stricken letter.	

Fade to:

Interior / RAF DEPOT, KARACHI, BARRACKS   Day

The same barracks on the inside, the door on another dusty and hot day. The breeze blows the net curtains from the doors. From behind the camera we can hear the occasional sounds of a car, a plane engine and soldiers at drill.

Lawrence sits at the desk writing a letter. He rocks on the chair, occasionally rises as he reads back his writing. A neatly-made bed is at the other side of the room. Music plays on the gramophone.

MUSIC: Beethoven Sonata No. 8 in C

> T.E. LAWRENCE V/O
> *Karachi. 15th January 1928. Dear Mrs Hardy, This is Sunday, and an hour ago I was on my bed, listening to Beethoven's last quartet: when one of the fellows came in and said that T.H. is dead. We finished the quartet, because all at once it felt like him: and now I am faced with writing something for you to receive three weeks too late.*

Cut to:

Interior / MAX GATE PARLOUR   Day

FLORENCE HARDY is dressed in mourning black and reads Lawrence's letter.

> T.E. LAWRENCE V/O
> *After your letter came at Christmas I wanted to reply: but a paragraph in the papers said that he was ill. Then I held my breath, knowing the tenuous balance of his life, which one cold wind would finish. For years he has been transparent with frailty.*
>
> *You, living with him, grew too used to it perhaps to notice it. It was only you who kept him alive all these years: you to whom I, amongst so many others, owed the privilege of having known him. And now, when I should grieve, for him and for you, almost it feels like a triumph.*
>
> *That day we reached Damascus, I cried, against all my control, for the triumphant thing achieved at last, fitly: and so the passing of T.H. touches me. He had finished and was so full a man.*

FLASHBACK: RUSSELL and FORSTER helping THOMAS HARDY on the steps in the Clouds Hill garden.

> T.E. LAWRENCE V/O (Continuing)
> *Each time I left Max Gate, having seen that, I used to blame myself for intruding upon a presence. But as you know I always came back the next chance I had. I think I'd have tried to come even if you had not been good to me: while you were very good: and T.H. So, actually, in his death I find myself thinking more of you. T.H. was infinitely bigger than the man who died three days back – and you were one of the architects.*

Page 35 of 120

Cut to:

Interior / RAF DEPOT, KARACHI, BARRACKS   **Day**

T.E. LAWRENCE V/O (Continuing)
A generation will pass before the sky will be perfectly clear of clouds for his shining. However, what's a generation to a sun? He is secure.

This is not the letter I'd like to write. You saw, though, how I looked on him, and guessed, perhaps, how I'd have tried to think of him, if my thinking had had the compass to contain his image.

Oh, you will be miserably troubled now, with jackal things that don't matter: you who have helped so many people, and whom therefore no one can help. I am so sorry. T. E. Shaw

Scene 9 – Letter from India – 3			
Location	RAF Depot, Karachi, India	**Est. Run Time**	03:00

Synopsis	
Lawrence writes again to Florence Hardy. He writes more on T.H.'s death, this time with more composure.	

Fade to:

Exterior / RAF KARACHI, BARRACKS   Night

The same barracks, outside. It is pitch black except for the light of a hurricane lamp which is has moths dancing around it. The camp is still except for the sounds of crickets, the occasional dog bark. The door to the office is open. It is a hot night. The breeze blows the net curtains from the doors. Lawrence sits in his chair; the back against the barracks wall. He again is writing a letter. He rocks on the chair, occasionally rises as he reads back his writing.   Music is plays on the gramophone on the desk inside the barracks and the sound gently fills the room.

MUSIC – Beethoven Moonlight Sonata

T.E. LAWRENCE V/O
Karachi. 16th February 1928. Dear Mrs Hardy, I'm afraid I wrote you a very poor letter, the day I heard that T.H. was gone. But just then the news struck me almost as a triumph. He had kept it up to the very end: and was through with an existence he had not highly valued. It may be rest, afterwards: whereas for you I could only see ●present sorrow and a sense of want.

T.E. LAWRENCE V/O (continuing)
So I was sorrier for you than for myself. T.H. was the most honourable stopping place I've ever found, and I shall miss him more and more. I wonder if you will be like that: or if time will make the being alone easier for you.

The music has ended and the needle plays the centre of the disk, making an increasingly annoying repetitive scratching sound. LAWRENCE rises from the chair and looks out into the night.

T.E. LAWRENCE V/O
Mrs. Shaw, who was at the Abbey, sent me a wonderful account of it.

LAWRENCE stretches and yawns and stifles a twinge of back ache. He folds the letter and walks into the barrack's hut and closes the door.

T.E. LAWRENCE V/O
These bodies of ours are very tiring silly things. Yours ever T, E Shaw.

A few seconds later the lamp in the hut dims and it is dark. There is silence for a few seconds then the silence is broken by the sound of gentle, sorrowful sobbing from LAWRENCE.

Scene 10 – Return to England

Location	Plymouth Harbour	Est. Run Time	03:00

Synopsis
Lawrence returns to England and is assigned to RAF Cattewater in Plymouth where he is commanded by his old friend Sydney Smith. Sydney, his wife Clare have been friends with T.E. for some years.

Fade to:

Newpaper - Front Page – Lawrence in Afghanistan.

NEWSREEL: LAWRENCE'S arrival back in England.

LAWRENCE, disembarking from a ship off Plymouth, from Gaumont Graphic newsreel.

CAPTION: February 1929, Plymouth

LAWRENCE has been recalled from India to England and assigned to an RAF base in Plymouth where he works with an old friend on RAF speedboats.

Cut to:

Exterior/PLYMOUTH HARBOUR   Day

LAWRENCE steps from a pilot boat onto the harbour steps. He climbs the steps where he is greeted by an RAF driver.

> DRIVER
> *Welcome home Mr Lawrence.*

> T.E. LAWRENCE
> *Mr Shaw. And thank you. Where to?*

> DRIVER
> *Strict orders sir. Straight to your quarters at Cattewater.*

Page 39 of 120

Scene 11 – An Old Friend

Location	RAF Cattewater Plymouth	Est. Run Time	03:00

Synopsis
Lawrence is assigned a new role
working with an old friend.

Cut to:

Interior / RAF CATTEWATER CO'S OFFICE   Day.

Lawrence takes a deep breath and opens the office door.
His face lights up as he recognizes his old friend who rises
from his chair to greet him.

> **T.E. LAWRENCE**
> *Sidney? My God how are you?*

LAWRENCE and SMITH exchange handshakes and hugs.

> **CO SYDNEY SMITH**
> *Ned! Did you have a pleasant trip home?*

> **T.E. LAWRENCE**
> *Not a word I would choose. Those bloody
> vultures filmed me coming off the ship.*

> **CO SYDNEY SMITH**
> *Yes; they got wind of your return because of the
> troubles in Afghanistan.*

> **T.E. LAWRENCE**
> *Ah quite. Heard I was a few miles away from it
> in Karachi and they put two and two together
> eh?*

> **CO SYDNEY SMITH**
> *Quite so; my God Ned; last time I saw you was
> in Cairo, 1922?*

Page 40 of 120

T.E. LAWRENCE
March 1921. How is Clare?

CO SYDNEY SMITH
She is very well and sends her regards.

T.E. LAWRENCE
You're not getting any younger you know.

CO SYDNEY SMITH
And you are as direct as ever! Do you ever hear from Winston?

T.E. LAWRENCE
We exchange a line or two.

CO SYDNEY SMITH
Well; he's the reason you're here. Wants me to keep an eye on you.

T.E. LAWRENCE
An eye?

CO SYDNEY SMITH
Yes; and I've got a job for you.

T.E. LAWRENCE
Sounds ominous.

CO SYDNEY SMITH
You're to be my assistant; initially I'd like your help organising the Schneider Trophy – a seaplane contest. And then we're trying to build some faster boats – for search and rescue and the like.

T.E. LAWRENCE
Speed, competition and engines! And good company! What more can a man want!

Dissolve to:

NEWSREEL: Montage of photographs of Lawrence and his work on the RAF Speedboats.

Scene 12 – Interference			
Location	RAF Cattewater Plymouth	**Est. Run Time**	03:00

Synopsis
Lawrence is confronted by Sydney Smith about his involvement in Ernest Thirtle's Bill to abolish the death penalty for cowardice.

Cut to:

Interior / RAF CATTEWATER CO'S OFFICE   Day

CAPTION: March 1930.

LAWRENCE knocks and opens the office door. SYDNEY SMITH looks ashen-faced behind his desk. LAWRENCE walks in and stands before him. SMITH and LAWRENCE are friends but SMITH is obviously angry.

> CO SYDNEY SMITH
> *Ned. You've been at it again?*

> T.E. LAWRENCE
> *At what?*

> CO SYDNEY SMITH
> *Communicating. Interfering. Agitating.*

> T.E. LAWRENCE
> *What I do best sir.*

> CO SYDNEY SMITH
> *Ned! Not with Ernest Thirtle Member of Parliament for Shoreditch you don't.*

> T.E. LAWRENCE
> *I have?*

CO SYDNEY SMITH
Don't be coy Ned. You have. He aims to abolish the death penalty for cowardice and desertion.

T.E. LAWRENCE
I understand that's his objective

CO SYDNEY SMITH
And you've been helping him. Causing all sorts of unwelcome interference. I know you're not bothered Ned but Whitehall have been bending my bloody ear for an hour! Surely you of all people understand the need for discipline and deterrent?

T.E. LAWRENCE
Not when the punishment in disproportionate to the crime. If indeed standing against stupidity can be regarded as such.

CO SYDNEY SMITH
Don't be such a bloody fool Ned! You'll be gratified that even your old friend Allenby is fighting Thirtle's Bill. If it gets through the Commons the Lords will hit it roundly into the long grass.

T.E. LAWRENCE
Then we will recover the ball and throw it back in play.

CO SYDNEY SMITH
Ned, we have known each other for many years. You have a habit of ~~always~~ stepping briskly into the spotlight. And the bridges you burnt in your youth have created powerful, dangerous enemies.

T.E. LAWRENCE (angrily)
*It's the bloody battles that keep me going!
Without them I would wither into the dust. I
would have even less to fight for.*

LAWRENCE takes a deep breath.

T.E. LAWRENCE (continuing calmly)
*There are two things I fear. An untruth and an
injustice. Surely to be executed for speaking out
against the madness is an injustice?*

SYDNEY SMITH nods; he can see LAWRENCE is right.

T.E. LAWRENCE (continuing)
*Sydney. I have been told many times that I am
my own worst enemy. That I am a "hero". A
"good man". I have also learnt that for evil to
triumph it is only enough for good men to do
nothing.*

*My intention is to continue to be a "good
man".*

LAWRENCE turns and walks from the office. SYDNEY
SMITH slaps the desk in exasperation.

Scene 13 – A VIP Visitor

Location	Cloud's Hill Cottage	Est. Run Time	07:00

Synopsis	
Lawrence is visited by Winston Churchill. He wishes to discuss a new role for Lawrence.	

Cut to:

Exterior / CLOUD'S HILL COTTAGE   Day

CAPTION: March 1935.

CAMERA is static; focused on the cottage drive.

Sounds of a motorbike slowing and arriving on the drive. LAWRENCE rides into shot and pulls onto the drive. He stops the bike by the cottage and dismounts. He walks to the door of the cottage which is open and stops. Something is wrong. He picks up a wooden stave propped against the wall and cautiously enters the cottage, stave in hand.

Cut to:

Interior / CLOUD'S HILL COTTAGE, STAIRS   Day

CAMERA view shows Lawrence at the bottom of the stairs looking around the ground floor. He begins climbing the stairs cautiously.

He stops and sniffs the air like a hound. He smiles; it is a scent he knows well. Less cautiously he walks up the stairs. Smoke billows from the study.

CAMERA is at LAWRENCE'S POV.

In the gloom a well-built man, dressed in a suit and bow tie is sitting on the leather sofa smoking a cigar. His shape we seem to recognize. Then he speaks; it is WINSTON CHURCHILL.

WINSTON CHURCHILL
Dangerous and troubling times Ned?

LAWRENCE relaxes and lays down the stave.

T.E. LAWRENCE
As unorthodox a visit as ever!

WINSTON CHURCHILL
For someone who enjoys danger I would have thought this was very much your "bag".

LAWRENCE lights the fire and candles. The room begins to fill with light.

T.E. LAWRENCE
Well, after a long drive from London I'm sure your visit was not social.

WINSTON CHURCHILL
Social, business and pleasure Lawrence. A fine bolt hole you have here. Perfect for retirement.

T.E. LAWRENCE
A place where someone called live out their lives in peace?

WINSTON CHURCHILL
*A little young for hanging up your **saif**?*

T.E. LAWRENCE
Perhaps. But then the military was always a means to an end. However, I shall not miss it.

WINSTON CHURCHILL
You will Ned. You will miss changing it. From the inside. What you need is stimulation. Something to exercise the mind and the soul as well as the body.

T.E. LAWRENCE
Are you offering me a position? Last time you sold me that post in the colonial office in 1921.

WINSTON CHURCHILL
Which you did with intelligence and not a little panache.

T.E. LAWRENCE
A role as an ambassador perhaps? Look pretty. Keep my mouth shut? No honour in that.

WINSTON CHURCHILL (somberly)
War is coming Lawrence. Dark clouds are gathering. The storm will gather shortly. Germany becomes ever more powerful. They are re-arming. Baldwin and Chamberlain don't agree but they are wrong. The Germans have reintroduced conscription. They are rebuilding their army. Baldwin thinks Hitler is at his beck and call. The relationship is quite the reverse.

T.E. LAWRENCE
Oh no Winston! No more bloody fighting. I've lived through enough nightmares for a thousand lifetimes

WINSTON CHURCHILL
There are other ways of fighting Ned; you've shown that many times. The next war will be won with intelligence.

T.E. LAWRENCE
Any one who starts a war shows no intelligence.

WINSTON CHURCHILL
Quite so; but in the commencement of such a situation you would agree that enemies must be engaged with whatever weapons we have at hand, be they physical or logical.

T.E. LAWRENCE
I would so agree.

WINSTON CHURCHILL
The Secret Service will be our weapon Lawrence. It is our nation's intelligence but in disarray. It is a private club for Cambridge gentlemen run by Kell and others to settle old scores. It needs new structure, a fresh focus. It needs leadership. It needs your mind.

T.E. LAWRENCE
The chivalrous white knight battling insubstantial dragons?

WINSTON CHURCHILL
Precisely. Your work in Arabia, your work in India, your work in Palestine, your approach and connections all helped in many ways. You have a talent for getting under the enemy's skin and understanding their motivations. Understanding the way the enemy think then finding the weapon – be it sword or pen – to combat the enemy. then ever

War is perhaps two, perhaps four years away. We need to grow our secret service armoury to be able to meet the Germans and their allies on the battlefield with dominant force. These are your talents Ned.
T.E. LAWRENCE
If that is what you call them.

WINSTON CHURCHILL
I do. And you would agree that retirement would be a criminal waste of those faculties?

LAWRENCE nods and turns his back on CHURCHILL leaning with both hands on the mantelpiece to listen.

T.E. LAWRENCE
You know how I hate waste.

WINSTON CHURCHILL
You have courage Lawrence. You can speak. You can listen. I have also seen you stand.

T.E. LAWRENCE
Perhaps more through fear then flight!

WINSTON CHURCHILL
Courage, Ned, is what it takes to stand and speak; sometimes courage is also what it takes to sit down and listen. Ned. I am building a team. an army *I need you to lead and direct it. It would co-ordinate Foreign Office, War Office, Air Ministry, Admiralty, Police and MI5. Leo Amery supports the approach. It would effectively merge MI5 and MI6.*

T.E. LAWRENCE
And if I decline. Is this an order?

WINSTON CHURCHILL
You're a civilian now; you have retired. You owe me no fealty. I cannot force you or order you. cajoul

T.E. LAWRENCE (smiles)
I know.

WINSTON CHURCHILL
But in your heart Ned, I also know you want to. You like challenges. You would want to find peace and be an ambassador for it. Save lives, diminish conflict.

LAWRENCE smiles. He examines the Aqaba grass plant on his mantelpiece.

T.E. LAWRENCE
Interesting. And the next step?

WINSTON CHURCHILL
Come up to London. Next week. Wednesday. Meet with Amery, McDonogh, Richard Meinertzhagen and myself. It's a pity we lost your old mentor David Hogarth.

T.E. LAWRENCE (swayed)
Still. All good men. Very good men. With many enemies.

CHURCHILL rises and smiles – he has convinced him. They shake hands.

WINSTON CHURCHILL
Haven't we all Ned. And in fighting our enemies we need to know them. Get behind them so to speak.

T.E. LAWRENCE
I would agree; I have already approached Henry Williamson – he's a good friend of Oswald Mosely.

WINSTON CHURCHILL
Ahead of the game as ever Ned. Enjoy your weekend.

They begin to descend the staircase.

Cut to:

Exterior / CLOUD'S HILL COTTAGE   Day

LAWRENCE and CHURCHILL walk from the cottage through the garden to the drive; a car as if from nowhere, pulls up.

WINSTON CHURCHILL
I hear rumours that that filmmaker Alex Korda wants to make a moving picture of your life?

Lawrence: A Silent Passing

T.E. LAWRENCE
Not if I can help it.

WINSTON CHURCHILL
You should star in it Ned. Hollywood would have been an excellent alternative vocation – a consummate actor. Your dramatic gestures, refusing knight hood, gallantry medals. You were born for the stage. Always backing into the limelight!

T.E. LAWRENCE
When it is my advantage to do so!

WINSTON CHURCHILL
Be careful Ned; I cannot control every ingredient of this dish you are preparing. You are being watched. Kell will certainly oppose you and you do seem to attract notoriety like bees around a honey pot.

T.E. LAWRENCE
I know. I will perhaps use the press to make the right noises.

WINSTON CHURCHILL
To have news value is to have a tin can tied to one's tail?

T.E. LAWRENCE
Then I shall have – news value. Who wrote, "the printing press is the greatest weapon in the armoury of the modern commander?"

WINSTON CHURCHILL
You Ned; as well you know!

WINSTON gets in the car and pulls away. Lawrence is left standing silently on the drive watching the car disappear down the lane.

Scene 14 – Confuse and Confound			
Location	Chartwell	**Est. Run Time**	00:30

Synopsis:
Churchill reads T.E. LAWRENCE'S announcement in the newspaper that he is to retire.

Cut to:

Exterior / CHARTWELL, TERRACE   Day

CAMERA shows WINSTON CHURCHILL on *the* ~~his~~ terrace of his home at Chartwell. He is eating his breakfast and reading the newspaper aloud.

> WINSTON CHURCHILL (reads)
> *It has been announced that Mr. T. E. Shaw, known as Lawrence of Arabia, currently an aircraftman in the Royal Air Force is to retire from active duty. It is his intention to enjoy his retirement in seclusion at his cottage, Cloud's Hill in Dorset. Mr Shaw asked that his privacy be respected..*

He looks up from his newspaper.

> WINSTON CHURCHILL (continuing)
> *Confuse and confound the enemy Ned! Confuse and confound 'em!*

He calls inside the house.

> WINSTON CHURCHILL (continuing)
> *Clemmie! Clemmie! You must come and read this! Highly entertaining!*

Fade to Next Scene.

Scene 15 – Letter to Florence			
Location	Cloud's Hill Cottage	**Est. Run Time**	01:30

Synopsis
Lawrence proof-reads a letter to
Florence Hardy.

Cut to:

Exterior / CLOUD'S HILL COTTAGE   Day

CAMERA shows T.E. LAWRENCE outside the door of
his cottage. He wears overalls and his motorbike is
parked close by.

He is reading and making final corrections to a letter
he is writing.

> T.E. LAWRENCE V/O
> *Clouds Hill, Easter Monday 1935. Dear
> Mrs Hardy, I am sorry I missed you the day
> you came – as also at Max Gate, a week
> after, when I tried in turn to find you. The
> Indiscretion proved charming. You have
> made a beautiful little book of it. I have
> enjoyed the reading, and enjoy the
> possession.*
>
> *Clouds Hill is going to be all right as a
> living place, I fancy. The last three weeks
> have almost been unbroken peace. I feel very
> indisposed to do anything more; and very
> tired.*

TE LAWRENCE V/O (continuing)
The rhododendron is in good flower at the moment. I hope you will be able to see it, some day. Except for Wednesday I shall be here continuously now, I hope, though in disorder, as the place is unfinished. But please come. Yours ever T E Shaw.

He nods his satisfaction and places the letter in an envelope and places the envelope inside his overalls.

He picks up the goggles hanging from the handlebars of the motorbike, mounts the motorbike and starts the engine.

He pulls down his goggles and rides away.

SOUND of motorbike disappearing down the lane.

Scene 16 – Joy of Freedom			
Location	Bovington Road	**Est. Run Time**	02:00

Synopsis
Lawrence enjoying the motor cycle ride into Wareham.

Cut to:

Exterior / BOVINGTON'S LANES   Day

MUSIC: Beethoven Symphony No. 9 – Choral - Ode for Joy.

CAMERA shows face on POV of Lawrence on his Brough Superior SS100 motorbike.

He is enjoying the ride, the freedom of the road. He is riding quickly but safely.

A tractor pulls out but he avoids and overtakes it easily.

For the first time in the story we see him obviously and totally overjoyed. [In his head ~~his~~ The sound-track is Beethoven's 9th – Choral – Ode for Joy.

Scene 17 – Surveillance

Location	Wareham South Street	Est. Run Time	02:00

Synopsis	
Lawrence shopping in Wareham. He is under surveillance.	

Cut to:

Exterior / WAREHAM SOUTH STREET   Day

CAMERA shows view of LAWRENCE arriving on his motorbike. He rides over the Frome Bridge by the Old Granary. He pulls up outside the Black Bear Hotel, parks and dismounts the bike.

Parked down the street is a black Wolseley car. Two men are inside it and watch as LAWRENCE walks down the street.

LAWRENCE purposefully enters the Post Office. His business done a few moments later he exits the Post Office and continues down the street. He stops and says "Good Morning" to a lady passer-by. They chat for a few moments. He points up the street to St Martin's Church and nods.

JOHN HANDLER an MI5 operative gets out of the car and closes the door. He is dressed in trilby, suit, tie and long black overcoat. He lights a cigarette and walks down the street towards where LAWRENCE is; he watches intently, obviously following and observing him.

LAWRENCE goes into the butcher and appears a few moments later with a small parcel of meat. He enters the barber shop and greets the owner. Through the window we can see he is getting a haircut. LAWRENCE seems not to have noticed he is being watched.

HANDLER walks back to the car and gets in.

> HANDLER (To PAGE)
> *We wait…*

Cut to:

Exterior / CLOUD'S HILL COTTAGE   Day

A few hours later the same day Lawrence returns.

CAMERA shows a REPORTER and PHOTOGRAPHER waiting outside the door of Cloud's Hill. They try the front door but it is locked.

SOUND of a motorbike approaching and LAWRENCE rides into view and parks the motorbike a few yards from the front door of the cottage. Immediately *the* PHOTOGRAPHER takes a photo of LAWRENCE on his motorbike and the REPORTER presses him for information.

> REPORTER
> *Mr Lawrence? Now you've announced your retirement what do you…..*

LAWRENCE swings his right hand and grabs the camera and throws it away where it smashes on the ground. With the left fist coming the other way he hits the reporter on the side of the head and the REPORTER falls to the ground. LAWRENCE is shaking with his own anger.

> T.E. LAWRENCE (losing control)
> *Leave me alone for God's sake! Leave me alone!*

The REPORTER and PHOTOGRAPHER run for it.

LAWRENCE leans against his front door and violently hits the wall with his fist and the anger dissipates. LAWRENCE steps back and looks at his bloodied and injured fist. He shows no pain. He looks at it as if it is someone else's hand. It's as if the incident hadn't happened LAWRENCE unlocks the door and walks into the cottage.

Scene 18 – Conspiracy

Location	War Office, Whitehall	Est. Run Time	02:00

Synopsis
Plots are in place to get rid of Lawrence lead by British Secret Service.

led the [handwritten]

Cut to:

Interior / WHITEHALL. KELL'S OFFICE   Day.

CAMERA shows view of a senior army officer; he stares from the window of the office. We do not see his face but do see he is a high-ranking officer.

A clock ticks in the darkened room. The officer casts a long shadow. The atmosphere is tense.

The officer is Major General Sir Vernon Waldegrave Kell – he is Head of MI5 – also known as "K".

Seated in the room are HANDLER and PETER PAGE.

> KELL (calmly)
> *You have done well Handler; we had suspected Churchill was behind the proposal and Lawrence had made a number of attempts to throw us off the scent. We know he has already visited leaders in Berlin. We must now decide what to do. And how to do it.*

> HANDLER
> *Do you believe his position will be confirmed?*

KELL
Without doubt. Winston will get his way on this one.

HANDLER
And this would change the game?

KELL
Without doubt. His appointment might mean a certain equilibrium will be upset.

KELL turns from the window – he is incandescent.

KELL (continuing)
We can't have a bloody sado-masochistic little queer leading the British Secret Service! Just like we will not allow a bloody playboy and an American divorcee to be King and Queen! Both are equally unacceptable.

HANDLER
Lawrence has fingers in all sorts of pies. The Zionists thinks he will spoil the party in Palestine. The Germans think of him as a master spy. He is a supporter of Indian Independence. His effect on MI5 and MI6 would be devastating. foreign policy?

KELL
Gentlemen. It will be some weeks before anything will come to fruition. For now we should watch and wait. See what develops. Find out what he is up to.

HANDLER (menacingly)
And if things do...?

HANDLER searches for the word, removing a piece of tobacco from his tongue.

HANDLER (continuing)
Develop?

KELL
Then we will willingly stride across that bridge when we are at its threshold.

CAMERA ~~goes~~ moves into close up on KELL and the intense determination in his eyes.

a bridge with a threshold ??

Scene 19 – Searching the Cottage			
Location	Bovington Heath, Dorset	**Est. Run Time**	02:30

Synopsis
Lawrence's Cottage is searched by Peter Page of MI5.

Fade to:

Exterior / BOVINGTON CAMP LANE   **Day**

CAPTION: 11th May 1935 at 2pm

A black Wolsely car approaches from the direction of Bovington Camp on the same lane where LAWRENCE will later have his accident.

It pulls up at the side of the road about 100 yards from the site of the accident just past where the army tents are pitched.

PETER PAGE exits the car on the left-hand side. He is dressed in a hat, suit and overcoat. He carries two brown paper parcels tied with string. He runs onto the heath land and the car pulls away immediately.

He finds a gorse thicket and finds a military green bin perhaps 2ft x 3ft x 1ft; it is obvious that he has been there before.

He opens the parcels and begins to change into clothes contained in the parcels.

He wraps up his clothes roughly in the parcels, ties the string loosely and places the parcels in the bin. He is now dressed in camouflage green trousers and jumper – he is almost dressed militarily. He creeps from the gorse bush and stealthily works his way across the heath trying to avoid being seen.

CAMERA POV is now at the top of the bank of rhododendrons looking down on Cloud's Hill Cottage. PAGE crouches down cautiously and views the cottage.

LAWRENCE is working on his motorbike filling the petrol tank with fuel. He puts the can back in the garage, closes the garage door, wipes his hands on a rag and puts on the goggles. He starts the bike and rides away.

FADING SOUND of motorbike driving into the distance, ~~which fades.~~

PAGE emerges from the rhododendrons and goes through the front door which is unlocked. He looks behind him and does not notice a piece of folded paper which has fallen from the door frame to the floor.

CAMERA POV is now at the door of the cottage.

PAGE runs upstairs and we hear him opening cupboards, moving about. He runs back down the stairs and goes into the room on the ground floor. There are a handful of letters in a rack. He takes one of the letters from its envelope and reads it.

> LADY ASTOR V/O
> *It would be wonderful to see you again. Your last visit was most entertaining. You would be most welcome to join a few guests at a weekend party including Mr Baldwin on Saturday 25th May at Cliveden. We understand there is a potential reorganisation of the forces proposed and would like to understand the upheaval. Yours Lady Nancy Astor.*

A reply has been clipped to it, not yet sent and he reads it.

> T.E. LAWRENCE V/O
> *My apologies, Lady Astor, but no. Neither Prime Minister nor wild mares would not at present take me from Clouds Hill. Also there is something broken in the works...*

PAGE picks up another. One is post-marked Barnstaple, Devon. He takes the letter from its envelope and reads it.

> HENRY WILLIAMSON V/O
> *I urge you to visit me at Barnstaple at your earliest opportunity. Oswald Mosely is keen for you to meet Hitler and Goebels next month perhaps in Berlin. War in Europe is seen by the National Socialists as inevitable but your input could bring about an environment of negotiation. Yours Henry Williamson·*

PAGE replaces the letters in the rack as he found them.

He Runs through the front door, treading on the piece of paper as he does so, back up the rhododendron bank and disappears into the thicket.

Scene 20 – Hidden on the Heath

Location	Bovington Heath, Dorset	Est. Run Time	02:30

Synopsis
Two junior officers in the ROAC walking their dog find Page's clothes

Cut to:

Exterior / BOVINGTON HEATH   Day

CAMERA shows the inside of the gorse bush where PAGE has changed and his clothes are hidden.

In the distance we can hear voices; two junior RAOC officers JOHN PRENTICE and DOUGLAS "MONTY" CAKE are walking a dog.

> JOHN PRENTICE (OFF CAMERA)
> *Gin! Gin!*

Gin the dog appears in the gorse bush and finds the bin; the lid falls of and she pulls out one of the parcels and barks. She paws the parcel.

> JOHN PRENTICE (OFF CAMERA)
> *Now what has that bloody dog found? At this rate we'll never get to camp in time for dinner. Where is that damned dog?*

> MONTY CAKE (OFF CAMERA)
> *Probably some rotting animal like last time. I think she shot in there.*

PRENTICE and CAKE appear in the gorse thicket. Gin is gradually opening one of the parcels.

JOHN PRENTICE
What have you got there Gin?

CAKE and PRENTICE unwrap the parcels. They find trousers, a hat, and a coat.

MONTY CAKE
Clothes. Some walker has left his clothes or some such.

JOHN PRENTICE
Bloody funny. What do you think?

CAMERA POV is from the edge of the pine forest. PAGE is hidden behind a fallen tree and watches the gorse thicket. He has seen that his clothes have been discovered.

MONTY CAKE (baffled)
Mystery if you ask me. Look. Lets put them back – there may be a logical explanation but we report it to the MPs when we get back to camp.

JOHN PRENTICE
Agreed. Strange, so close to camp. Yes, come on, look at the time. We're late already.

MONTY examines the hat. There is a name tag on it.

MONTY CAKE
Hang on John; look a name. Peter Page? Well at least a name to give to the MPs.

They rewrap the clothes and place them back into the bin. They put Gin on a lead.

CAMERA POV is from the edge of the pine forest. PAGE watches as they emerge from the gorse thicket. MONTY and JOHN look around. No one to be seen they continue their walk.

Once out of sight PAGE runs into the thicket and hurriedly gets changed into his civvies.

CAMERA POV is ~~from~~ 20 yards from the gorse thicket.

PAGE emerges with the bin. He throws it as far as he can and it lands in a ditch.

He looks around. He has not been seen and walks back to the road.

As he arrives at the ~~same~~ spot where he was dropped off the same black car reappears as if by magic.

He gets into the passenger seat of the car and it pulls away.

Cut to:

Interior / WOLSELEY CAR   Day

> HANDLER (scrambling)
> *So. Page. What did those blood-hound senses of yours sniff out?*

PAGE is sweating and nervous.

> PETER PAGE
> *Looks like you were right. He's talking to the Black Shirts. They're setting him up to meet Hitler next month.*

> HANDLER
> *Henry Williamson?*

> PETER PAGE (nervously)
> *Just so. This is getting out of hand. If he meets Mosely and Hitler war may not be as sure as we would like it to be.*

carried

> HANDLER (ominously)
> *And we can't allow that can we?*

HANDLER feigns concern.

> HANDLER (continuing)
> *They may begin to negotiate.*

> PETER PAGE
> *And?*

> HANDLER
> *And? And we should report back to Kell in London.*

Looks at PAGE who is sweating. PAGE takes out a silver hip flask from the glove box in the dashboard. As he opens the box we see a pistol. He takes a swig of liquor and puts the hip flash back in the glove box.

HANDLER slaps PAGE on the knee.

> HANDLER (brightly)
> *Relax old boy. We'll be back in London by the evening. And I know a charming little pub on the edge of the New Forest where we can top you up again.*

Scene 21 – Mystery Deepens			
Location	Bovington Camp, Dorset	**Est. Run Time**	01:30

Synopsis
Prentice and Cake report their find.

Cut to:

Interior / BOVINGTON MILITARY POLICE   Day

Later the same day, early evening PRENTICE and CAKE are standing in the office talking to a SERGEANT in the Military Police who is pre-occupied with paperwork. GIN is occasionally barking annoyingly.

SERGEANT
So you saw a bunch of old clothes dumped in a gorse bush.

JOHN PRENTICE
No, they were not old. They were used and of good quality.

SERGEANT (dismissively)
Probably some old tramp nicked them, hid 'em there and your old dog dug 'em out. Perhaps a local old biddy using it as a drop box for a friend to pick up. Kids?

MONTY CAKE
It was just damned peculiar. And there was a name in the hat. Peter Page.

>SERGEANT (scratching his head)
>*Peter Page? No. Not a name I know.*

>JOHN PRENTICE
>*Look aren't you going to write it down?*

MP SERGEANT is pushed into a corner. Reluctantly. He takes a sheet of paper. And writes a few notes.

>SERGEANT (reluctantly)
>*Peter Page. There. Happy?*

PRENTICE and CAKE look decidedly unhappy.

>SERGEANT (continuing)
>*Look why don't you go back out before it goes dark, get the clothes parcels and bring them back? At least we would have some physical evidence.*

>JOHN PRENTICE (looking at his watch)
>*We do have time.*

With a nod at each other and GIN in tow they hurry from the MP Office. As they go out of sight the MP SERGEANT screws up the paper and throws it deftly in the bin.

>SERGEANT
>*Couple of bloody boy scouts....*

>**Cut to:**

Exterior / BOVINGTON HEATH, GORSE THICKET

It is sunset, the light is fading. PRENTICE and CAKE arrive at the gorse thicket and go inside. They emerge a few seconds later empty handed.

>JOHN PRENTICE (frustrated)
>*Nothing. No clothes. No bin. Look old man I've had enough mysteries for one day. The MPs have it in their little black book. We've reported it and done our duty.*

MONTY CAKE

Quite so; bloody waste of time. Come on Prentice; let's see if we can get back to camp in time to down a pint or two in the mess before bedtime.

CAMERA PANS DOWN so we see the bin in a ditch as the men walk away.

Scene 22 – Not Liked			
Location	Hotel, London	**Est. Run Time**	02:00

Synopsis
Handler and Page confirm actions to eliminate Lawrence.

Cut to:

Interior / HOTEL ROOM, LONDON   Night.

PAGE pours himself a stiff whiskey, his hand shakes as he pours it.

HANDLER is sat on the bed, relaxed and lying down. He is on the phone to KELL.

PAGE only half listens; he already knows what is to come.

> HANDLER
> *Yes sir, I understand sir. We'll liaise with operations if we need anything. And the timing? As soon as possible? Certainly sir, that's what we were planning. Thank you sir. I'll call tomorrow to confirm success. Good night to you sir.*

HANDLER gently puts down the phone on the bedside. He kicks his shoes off, puts his hands behind his head and wiggles his toes.

> HANDLER (continuing)
> *Well Page, England's most famous and courageous queer is not liked. Not liked at all.*

HANDLER (Continuing)
We need to pick up a few things and go back very early tomorrow morning. Kell has given his blessing.

Come on let's get you down to the restaurant. This place does the most wonderful beef en croute and you look like you need feeding up.

PAGE looks very worried. He rises from his chair and knocks back his whiskey. HANDLER picks up his coat and they leave the hotel room.

Scene 23 – Final Hours			
Location	Clouds Hill Cottage Camp Post Office	**Est. Run Time**	02:30

Synopsis	
Lawrence's final hours. He is visited by the ghost of his old friend Sharif Ali who has died in 1931. He sends a parcel and telegram to his friend, author Henry Williamson.	

Cut to:

Interior / CLOUD'S HILL COTTAGE. STUDY   Day

CAPTION 13th May 1935 at 10:45am

LAWRENCE is sleeping on the sofa in the Cloud's Hill study. He is dreaming.

In his dream he sees his old friend SHARIF ALI, attired in full Arab dress materialise in his sitting room/study in front of the fireplace. The ghost of SHARIF ALI is an impressive sight. SHARIF ALI bows and gestures a greeting to him. SHARIF ALI and LAWRENCE exchange words in Arabic. LAWRENCE remains asleep but a little restless as he sleeps.

SUBTITLES: translation into English.

> SHARIF ALI (grandly)
> *As-Salamu Alaykum*

> T.E. LAWRENCE
> *Wa-Alaykum As-Salaam*

SHARIF ALI
Lam naraka mundhu muddah

SUBTITLE: *It's been a long time.*

SHARIF ALI steps towards LAWRENCE.

T.E. LAWRENCE
Eshtakto elaika

SUBTITLE: *I've missed you so much.*

SHARIF ALI
Ta'ala Ourance

SUBTITLE: *Come with me Lawrence*

T.E. LAWRENCE
Matha? Ayn?

SUBTITLE: *What? Where?*

SHARIF ALI (comfortingly)
LaTaklak. Bayt.

SUBTITLE: *Don't worry. Home.*

T.E. LAWRENCE (pleased)
Inshallah. Shokran Sadeek.

SUBTITLE: *If Allah wishes it. Thank you friend.*

SHARIF ALI bows in farewell.

SHARIF ALI
Araka Oorance.

SUBTITLE: *Until later Lawrence.*

Page 74 of 120

SHARIF ALI takes another step towards him and his ghost and ~~the~~ dream dissolves.

LAWRENCE wakes with a start from his dream. He opens his eyes and stares around the empty room a little disconcerted.

He gets up from the sofa. He is a little disoriented. He goes to the bathroom and washes his face in a bowl of water and dries it. A few minutes pass.

Cut to:

Exterior / CLOUD'S HILL COTTAGE   Day.

CAPTION 13th May 1935 at 11:15

LAWRENCE steps from the front door of the cottage. He is about to mount his motorbike and sees the paper from his front door. He picks it up, puts it in his pocket and smiles. Someone has been in the cottage.

He mounts his motorbike, starts the engine and rides off for what will be the last time.

As the sound disappears the cottage garden is left in silence and we dwell for a few seconds on the garden. A few minutes pass.

Cut to:

Exterior / BOVINGTON CAMP POST OFFICE   Day.

LAWRENCE pulls up on his motorbike outside the Post Office. He is wearing his blue overalls. He switches off the bike, dismounts and hangs the goggles on the handle bars.

The goggles catch the sunlight and flash as they swing on the handlebars.

He takes a small parcel of books from the saddle bag and a piece of paper from his inside pocket and walks into the Post Office.

Cut to:

Interior / BOVINGTON CAMP POST OFFICE Day

LAWRENCE enters and places the books on the counter. He draws the telegram from his inside pocket.

> POST MASTER
> *Morning Mr Shaw; beautiful day sir!*

> T.E. LAWRENCE (distracted)
> *Yes, beautiful. I have these books and a telegram to send to the same address in Devon.*

> POST MASTER
> *Henry Williamson; Shallowford Filleigh, Devon. I got relatives in Devon you know.*

I've got

> T.E. LAWRENCE (To POSTMASTER)
> *Let me just check the telegram again.*

> T.E. LAWRENCE V/O
> *Lunch Tuesday Wet Fine Cottage One Mile North Bovington Camp. Shaw.*

LAWRENCE hands it to the POST MASTER who checks the telegram.

> POST MASTER
> *Certainly sir; I'll send the parcel this afternoon and the telegram right away.*

LAWRENCE places a couple of coins on the post office counter.

> T.E. LAWRENCE (lightly)
> *Thank you. Have a good day. Should be fine I hope!*

LAWRENCE walks out of the Post Office.

Cut to:

Exterior / BOVINGTON CAMP POST OFFICE   Day.

LAWRENCE walks from the Post Office and takes the goggles from the handlebars. He mounts and starts the motorbike, adjusts the goggles and rides away, back towards the cottage.

Outside the Post Office there is a man, dressed in an overcoat, in the Public Telephone Box. He is on the telephone and watches LAWRENCE depart. We do not hear we he says but says a few words and puts down the receiver. *we can see he*

CAMERA PANS to bright blue sky.

Scene 24 – Accident: Another Perspective

Loca tion	Bovington Camp Road	Est. Run Time	07:00

Synopsis
The scene shows and repeats with relevant additions the suspicious circumstances of T.E.'s motorcycle accident. It includes the black car, witnesses and the two delivery boys on bicycles with whom he collides.

Cut to:

Exterior / BLUE SKY   Day

CAPTION: 13th May 1935 at 11:25am Bovington, Dorset

CAMERA PANS from sun and sky to a deserted country lane lined with gorse bushes and pine tress, typical Dorset heath land. The long strip of black road stretches off in a straight line into the horizon. The road, though straight has a few dips in it.

Cut to:

Exterior / COUNTRY LANE, BOVINGTON   Day

T.E. LAWRENCE is riding at speed down the lane. Beethoven is playing in his head. Perhaps 400 yards in front of him he can see two boys on bicycles. A little way in front of that there is a glint of sun on glass; a car is approaching.

Cut to:

Exterior / COUNTRY LANE, BOVINGTON   Day

On the country lane two boys on old black delivery bicycles come into view. They are pedaling slowly and enjoying the day weaving a little on the empty road.

FRANK FLETCHER
Come on Albert! Keep up! We're never going to get to Moreton Woods at this rate!

ALBERT HARGRAVES
All right Frank; I'm pedaling as fast as a can! This bike weighs a ton!

FRANK
Anymore deliveries?

ALBERT (shouts)
Nah. That's it for today. We should still have plenty of time for collecting nests.

Behind them is the distant sound of a motorbike coming towards them at speed.

The boys continue to pedal and are almost side by side. FRANK is slightly in front. They are chatting and are more concerned with their plans than the road. Sub ~~Unconsciously~~ they move to single file with FRANK in front of ALBERT. Coming towards them in the opposite direction is a black car. A 1934 Wolsely 21/60. The boys do not notice it.

Cut to:

Exterior / COUNTRY LANE, BOVINGTON   Day

T.E. LAWRENCE is now perhaps 100 yards from the boys, *who are* now in single file. A black car is coming towards him; it is very close to the middle of the road.

A few hundred yards ahead of the boys on the right-hand side of the lane is a cluster of 20 army tents ~~camped~~ on the heath. The camp is a hive of activity with cooking fires, a game of cricket, soldiers lazing in the sun.

pitched

Cut to:

Exterior / BOVINGTON LANE, CAMP FENCE   Day

see page 11 .

On the edge of the camp walking along the low boundary fence looking towards the road is a soldier smoking a cigarette. It is CORPORAL ERNEST CATCHPOLE.   Above the sound of the car CATCHPOLE can also hear the sound of the motorbike coming towards him.

SLOW MOTION. The black car passes him at speed traveling at approximately 60 miles per hour. It is almost driving in the centre of the road. CATCHPOLE very briefly sees the driver and the passenger in the back seat on the driver's side. They look suspicious; intense. They are both dressed smartly, wearing a trilby hat, pinstriped suit and tie.

EXTREME SLOW MOTION. Frame by frame, as the car passes ahead of him, now level with the boys CATCHPOLE sees the car door open slightly. The passenger, PAGE, looks like he is about to get out of the car. It is something he can't explain. Just not right.

The car disappears into the dip in the road.

Cut to:

Exterior / COUNTRY LANE, BOVINGTON   Day

MUSIC – Beethoven Symphony No. 7 in A Major Allegretto.

Page 80 of 120

SLOW MOTION - LAWRENCE is now level with the car. Its rear passenger door on the driver's side is open. The door clips the handlebars and hits the petrol tank on the motorbike.

T.E. LAWRENCE begins to lose control of the bike. The car disappears into the distance and drives away at speed.

Cut to:

Exterior / BLUE SKY   Day

A "beat" of a second. All is peace and calm.

Cut to:

Exterior / COUNTRY LANE, BOVINGTON   Day

LAWRENCE'S black Brough Superior SS100 motorcycle GW 2275 appears from the dip in the road coming towards the boys and CATCHPOLE. The motorcycle is ridden by LAWRENCE who is wearing goggles, blue overalls but no helmet. The bike is seriously out of control weaving all over the road. We see the eyes of T.E. LAWRENCE; they are wide and frightened.

The motorbike careers into ALBERT'S bike who is in turn pushed into the back wheel of FRANK'S bike.

CORPORAL CATCHPOLE throws away his cigarette and runs towards the accident. ALBERT falls from his bike and is thrown a few yards from it. He is still. A few coins, coppers from his pocket, tumbles into the tarmac.

SOUND: Slow motion coins falling to the ground ~~almost~~ surreal.

FRANK falls from his bike. He dusts himself off and gets up almost immediately.

LAWRENCE is thrown over the handle bars of the motorbike and he slides down the road with huge force. The momentum carries him and the bike down the road. The bike ends up behind him. His head hits the tree and he ends up against the tree, propped up against it in a sitting position.

FRANK runs past ALBERT who is moving his legs (he is alive) and over to where LAWRENCE is against the tree. He arrives a moment before CATCHPOLE and they stand before LAWRENCE. Other soldiers from the camp begin to run up the road and towards the accident scene.

Through a strange desert-heat haze LAWRENCE can see the boy (FRANK) with the sun behind him. He ~~imagines it is~~ an Arab boy that he recognises.

[handwritten margin note: mistakes him for]

His eyes begin to glaze over as his head is gradually being covered with blood from his crown to his neck until only his intense blue eyes are visible.

His eyes now stare fixed towards the cloudless blue sky.

> T.E. LAWRENCE (whispering, breathlessly)
> *Dahoum?*

LAWRENCE'S eyes mist over, his lids flutter and close and he loses consciousness.

Dahoum (Selim Ahmed)
Photo taken by TEL

Lawrence in Dahoum's Clothes
Photo taken by Dahoum

Scene 25 – Still Hanging On			
Location	Bovington Camp Hospital	**Est. Run Time**	02:00

Synopsis
The scene shows Lawrence fighting for his life in the hospital intensive care.

Cut to:

Interior / CAMP HOSPITAL, INTENSIVE CARE   Day

CAPTION: 13th May 1935 at 1:30pm

CAMERA is at the door of a hospital room. Doctors and nurse come in and out of view. They are working to save the life of a man. On the bed T.E. LAWRENCE, his head bandaged is on oxygen. His breathing is shallow.

CAMERA PANS back looking down the corridor from the room to a set of double hospital doors. A plain clothes MI5 operative is guarding the door.

The door opens and HANDLER walks towards the room. He watches for a few moments trying to gauge the seriousness of the patient's condition. After a few moments he turns and walks back down the corridor.

Cut to:

Interior / BOVINGTON CAMP – AN OFFICE   Day.

HANDLER enters an empty office as if he owns the place and picks up the phone. He requests a number.

> HANDLER
> *Whitehall 278. Sir? Yes, the security lock down is in place. For at least the next 48 hours. Yes.*

HANDLER (continuing)
*Press blackout also - Special "D" notices
have been posted. Not even the nurses know
who he is. Of course; we've closed down the
cottage as well; Secret documents; that sort
of thing. How is he? Critical. Still hanging
on. He's a fighter I'll give him that. Good
news is that if he survives he'll probably be
unable to speak anyway.*

*Let us hope that for once Allah is not on his
side.*

Cut to:

Interior / CAMP HOSPITAL, INTENSIVE CARE   Day

CAPTION: 13th May 1935 at 8pm.

CAMERA is at the bedside. Lawrence looks stable and is
on a respirator which rhythmically keeps its time.

All is silent except for the rhythmic sound of the
respirator.

font size

Lawrence: A Silent Passing

Find & replace 'hanger' with 'hangar'

Scene 26 – Mechanically Sound			
Location	Bovington – A Hanger	**Est. Run Time**	02:00
Synopsis The scene shows Handler ensuring Brough's evidence does not compromise the conspiracy.			

Cut to:

Interior / BOVINGTON CAMP – A HANGER   Day

CAPTION: 14th May 1935 at 3pm

CAMERA shows HANDLER smoking a cigarette in the centre of a large and empty aircraft hanger except for the wreckage of Lawrence's bike on its stand.

SOUND of a motorbike approaching. The bike is also a Brough and is ridden through the hanger doors and stops a few yards from HANDLER.

The rider is GEORGE BROUGH the maker of Lawrence's bike. He turns off the bike, dismounts and removes his goggles and gloves.

They introduce themselves with a hand shake. *one word*

> GEORGE BROUGH
> *George Brough; I came as soon as I heard.*

> HANDLER
> *Fine machines you make Mr Brough.*

> GEORGE BROUGH
> *Quite so. And you are?*

> HANDLER *(evasively)*
> *I work for the Government.*

Page 85 of 120

GEORGE BROUGH
What can I do for you?

HANDLER
We just need you to examine the bike and confirm that it is mechanically sound.

GEORGE BROUGH
Certainly. Give me a few moments.

BROUGH kneels down, examines and tests brakes, wheels, chain etc. Immediately notices the dent on the petrol tank, black paint on the tank and handle bars. He nods having completed the inspection.

HANDLER
And?

GEORGE BROUGH
Of course it's mechanically sound! The bike has been struck by something – you can clearly see the black paint and the damage to the tank and the handle bars.

HANDLER (shrugs, feigns surprise)
We had established that it was damaged on its impact with the road.

GEORGE BROUGH
Nonsense man! The bike slid on the other side; you can see where the chrome has been scratched.

HANDLER
Purely supposition, Mr Brough. Mr Brough, in our investigation we only need to know if the machine was mechanically sound.

GEORGE BROUGH
But that was not the cause of the accident!

HANDLER.
The cause will be judged by our government engineers.

GEORGE BROUGH
Look. I don't know who you are but Lawrence was the finest rider I have ever met. On the many times I rode with him I can clearly state that he was most considerate to other road users. I never saw him take a single risk or put any other road user at the slightest inconvenience. I cannot believe nor accept Lawrence could have made an error. It is clear to me that given the marks of impact the bike was struck by something.

HANDLER
Mr Brough. Your business is a successful one is it not. I'm sure you wish it to remain so?

HANDLER puts a comforting hand on his shoulder.

HANDLER (continuing, menacingly)
Surely you do not want our engineers to suggest that a Brough motorbike, one of your motorbikes could have had any potential fault.

GEORGE BROUGH looks at HANDLER. He recognises the threat. He is worried and cornered.

HANDLER smiles. He drops his cigarette and puts it out with his foot. He smears it on the hanger floor.

HANDLER
So. The motorbike was mechanically sound?

BROUGH repeats the statement with the same rhythm but with no conviction.

> GEORGE BROUGH (resigned)
> *The motorbike was mechanically sound.*

> HANDLER (pleased)
> *Thank you Mr Brough; your help has been invaluable. Good day to you sir.*

HANDLER walks out of the hanger through the hanger doors. BROUGH is left standing dejectedly scratching his head looking at Lawrence's bike. There is nothing more he can do. He puts on his goggles and gloves, mounts his bike, starts it and rides away.

Scene 27 – Coaching the Witnesses

Location	Bovington – Police Station	Est. Run Time	02:00

Synopsis The scene shows Page ensuring the boy's evidence does not compromise the conspiracy.	

Cut to:

Interior / BOVINGTON CAMP – POLICE STATION   Day

CAPTION: 18th May 1935 at 11am

CAMERA shows PAGE walking confidently through the double doors of the Police Station.

He flashes his identity card and takes the POLICE SERGEANT to one side.

There is a short conversation; PAGE shakes the officer's hand and presses a wadge of five pound notes into it who accepts it nervously.

PETER PAGE walks into the office. The clock on the wall reads 11:00. Two boys are sitting looking very worried as PAGE enters.

Time passes;

The clock now shows 11:55. The door opens and PAGE walks out. As he passes the Police Sergeant he tips his hat.

> PETER PAGE
> *Thank you officer! My colleague and I may be back tomorrow.*

PAGE continues walking purposefully out of the building.

Scene 28 – A Silent Passing

Location	Bovington Hospital–Intensive Care	Est. Run Time	02:00

Synopsis

The doctor, Captain Allen examining Lawrence for signs of life and pronouncing his death.

BBC announces the death with Allenby broadcasting his obituary.

Cut to:

Interior / HOSPITAL INTENSIVE CARE   Day

CAPTION: 19th May 1935 at 8:25am

CAMERA shows CAPTAIN ALLEN in a white coat examining LAWRENCE on the bed for signs of life. He checks his pulse, eyelids, listens to his heart with a stethoscope.

CAPT ALLEN looks at the nurse and shakes his head.

> CAPTAIN ALLEN
> *It's all over now.*

CAPTAIN ALLEN pulls the sheet over LAWRENCE'S face.

LAWRENCE is laid gently on a hospital trolley; he is covered with a sheet and gently, reverently wheeled down the corridor by a PORTER.

The trolley reaches the outside double doors and stops. The PORTER looks at the weather, it is a grey miserable day and it is raining gently.

The PORTER crosses the courtyard with the trolley and enters the chapel.

SOLDIER

A ~~PORTER~~ is waiting for him. The SOLDIER takes control of the trolley, the PORTER departs and the SOLDIER wheels the trolley and lines it up so LAWRENCE is parallel to the altar.

the SOLDIER

From under his arm, ~~he~~ takes a Union Flag and drapes it over the body. He salutes and leaves the chapel. The body is alone.

Over this action we hear the news of LAWRENCE'S death read by the BBC NEWSREADER followed by the obituary of VISCOUNT ALLENBY originally broadcast by the BBC on the 19th May 1935.

> ALVAR LIDELL V/O (BBC newsreader)
> *We regret to announce the death of Mr. T. E. Shaw, Lawrence of Arabia, which occurred shortly after eight o'clock yesterday morning in Wool Military Hospital, Bovington Camp, Dorset. Mr. Shaw, who until recently was an aircraftman in the Royal Air Force, was injured in a motor-cycling accident on Monday night and did not recover consciousness. Tragic as it is that such a remarkable career should have been ended by a simple road accident, an official statement issued yesterday shows that if his fight for life had succeeded it would still have been a tragedy, for Mr. Shaw's brain was irreparably damaged. Mr. Shaw was 46 years of age.*
>
> VISCOUNT ALLENBY V/O
> *In T.E. SHAW, better known to the public as Colonel T.E. Lawrence - I have lost a good friend and valued comrade. When I first met him – in the summer of 1917 – he had just returned from some venturesome raid behind the Turkish front; thence force we were closely associated with the campaigns of 1917 and 1918 in Palestine and Syria – closely in mind and purpose, though distance often separated us widely.*

VISCOUNT ALLENBY (continuing)
Lawrence was under my command but after being acquainted with the strategic plan he had a free hand. His co-operation was marked by the utmost loyalty and I never had anything but praise for his work, which was invaluable.

NEWSREEL: Lawrence and Arab Army in the Desert

He was the mainspring of the Arab movement. He knew their language, their manners, their mentality; he understood their merry, sly humour: in daring, he led them; in endurance, he equalled, if not surpassed, their strongest. Though in complete sympathy with his companions, and sharing to the full with them hardship and danger, he was careful to maintain the dignity of his position as Confidential Advisor to the Emir Feisal. Himself an Emir, he wore the robes of that rank, and kept up a suitable degree of state.

His own bodyguard – men of wild and adventurous spirit – were picked by Lawrence personally. Mounted on thoroughbred camels they followed him in all his daring rides; and among those reckless desert rangers there was none who would not willingly have died for their chief. The shy and retiring scholar, archaeologist, philosopher, was swept by the tide of war into a position undreamt of.
His well-balanced brain and disciplined imagination facilitated adaptation to the new environment; and there shone forth a tactician, with a genius for leadership. Such men win friends – such also find critics and detractors. But the highest reward for success is the inward knowledge that it has been rightly won.

VISCOUNT ALLENBY V/O (Continuing)
Praise or blame were regarded with indifference by Lawrence. He did his duty as he saw it before him. He left, to us who knew and admired him, a beloved memory; and to countrymen, the example of a life well spent in the service.

WINSTON CHURCHILL V/O
In Colonel Lawrence we have lost one of the greatest beings of our time. I had the honour of his friendship. I knew him well. I hoped to see him quit his retirement and take a commanding part in facing the dangers which now threaten this country. No such blow has befallen the Empire for many years as his untimely death.

Cut to:

Exterior / BOVINGTON CAMP COURTYARD   Day

CAMERA shows HANDLER leaning against a wall. He watches as the SOLDIER marches back across the courtyard to the barracks.

HANDLER (unemotionally)
So. The Prince Orrance is dead.

HANDLER flicks away his cigarette and walks casually back into the main building.

Scene 29 – The Right Decision

Location	Bovington Camp - Captain Hyde-Pierce's Office	Est. Run Time	02:30

Synopsis
Handler ensures that Catchpole's evidence is not compromising.

Cut to:

Interior / CAMP - HYDE-PIERCE'S OFFICE Day

CAPTION: 19th May 1935 at 2pm

CAMERA shows CAPTAIN HYDE-PIERCE and HANDLER seated in an army office. There is a knock on the door.

>CAPTAIN HYDE-PIERCE
>*Come!*

CORPORAL CATCHPOLE marches in, salutes and stands to attention. HYDE-PIERCE is reading a buff folder.

>CAPTAIN HYDE-PIERCE
>*Catchpole, Corporal 7581979. Exemplary record. The inquest for Mr T.E. Shaw is tomorrow. You are to give evidence.*

>CORPORAL ERNEST CATCHPOLE
>*Sir.*

>CAPTAIN HYDE-PIERCE
>*And your evidence?*

CATCHPOLE
I witnessed the accident sir. I observed a black car; as it passed Shaw's motorbike I thought it glanced the motorbike with the…

CAPTAIN HYDE-PIERCE
Thought man! You're not paid to think! You're paid to observe and report.

CATCHPOLE (reasonably)
Permission to ask a question sir? If Shaw retired from active service two months since why is this a military matter?

CAPTAIN HYDE-PIERCE
Bloody impertinence! It's none of your damned….

HANDLER restrains HYDE-PIERCE.

HANDLER (cutting in)
And that is why I am here Corporal Catchpole. Mr Shaw was privy to a number of official secrets. It's important for national security that these are not compromised. It is imperative that any potential risks are properly managed.

CATCHPOLE is silent. He bites his lip. A potential stalemate.

HANDLER
Can I make a suggestion?

CAPTAIN HYDE-PIERCE shrugs disinterestedly; he is not interested in compromise.

HANDLER (forcefully)
Catchpole is an excellent officer and I know he would want no doubt attached to his character.

HANDLER (continuing)
No stain on such an exemplary record. He merely needs to state what he saw. That he saw the car pass the bike. Simple.

CATCHPOLE (reasonably)
But surely sir it's imperative the inquest have all the facts?

HANDLER
And so they will. And of course given such an exemplary record and a sound testimony I'm sure that he can be assured promotion, increased remuneration to pay for his beautiful baby daughter and his wife Georgina and of an excellent future career in the army. He just needs to...make the right decision.

CATCHPOLE gulps – it is a veiled threat. Even the CAPTAIN HYDE-PIERCE looks taken aback by the approach.

HANDLER (threateningly)
If of course his testimony is less than sound. There are any number of long-term postings to which his talents can be applied anywhere in the Empire.

CATCHPOLE bites his lip. A clear choice. Conscience, his family or truth.

HANDLER (continuing)
So.

HANDLER stands. As he does so he slaps his legs. He walks behind CATCHPOLE. He almost whispers in his ear.

>   HANDLER (continuing)
>   *Can you "make the right decision"?*
>
>   CATCHPOLE (under duress)
>   *I observed the motorbike pass the car.*
>
>   HANDLER
>   *You "observed the motorbike pass the car".*

HANDLER repeats the statement word by word. He smiles, victorious. He turns to HYDE_PIERCE.

>   HANDLER (continuing)
>   *Officer material this one I'm sure.*
>
>   CAPTAIN HYDE-PIERCE
>   *Dismissed.*

CATCHPOLE, salutes, turns and marches out. He knows he has been compromised and has made a "choice".

HANDLER and CAPTAIN HYDE-PIERCE rise to part. HANDLER puts a hand on HYDE-PIERCE'S elbow steering him to the door.

>   HANDLER
>   *I'm eternally grateful for your help with this one; you would not believe the flap that this would have created. Would you mind awfully if I make bold of your office and telephone my commander in Whitehall?*
>
>   CAPTAIN HYDE-PIERCE
>   *Certainly. I'm glad to be of assistance.*

HYDE-PIERCE is ushered out of his own office.

>   HANDLER
>   *Whitehall 278. Thank you. Yes sir. The place is still locked down, guards are at Cloud's Hill, and Special Branch are also outside the camp.*

HANDLER (Continuing)
Yes sir, Page has squared up the boys, the evidence from Brough only states the vehicle was roadworthy and Catchpole has buckled. Yes sir. I think we're in the clear. The coroner? A Neville Jones. Ex-army. I think we can rely on him to play a straight bat. Yes sir. Thank you sir.

HANDLER puts the phone down and taps the top of the telephone in satisfaction.

Cut to:

Interior / BOVINGTON CAMP – CHAPEL   Day

CAMERA shows LAWRENCE lying under a Union Flag in front of the altar.

ALVAR LIDELL V/O *(BBC newsreader)*
The funeral of Mr. T. E. Shaw, formerly Colonel Lawrence, will take place at Moreton Church, Dorset, at 2.30pm on Tuesday. The service will be a simple one and no mourning and no flowers are requested. Apart from those specially invited the service will be confined to his particular friends and those who were associated with him in Arabia. It is understood that there will be no military escort.

Scene 30 – The Inquest			
Location	Bovington Camp– Court Room	**Est. Run Time**	10:00

Synopsis
Inquest into the death of Mr T.E. Shaw. It is obvious Neville-Jones is "going through the motions". The boys have been coached. Catchpole is guarded with his answers. The jury is guided to the verdict. The black car is ignored.

Cut to:

Interior / BOVINGTON CAMP – COURT ROOM   Day

CAPTION: 21st May 1935 at 9am

CAMERA shows an empty court room – like a Village Hall.

TIMELAPSE as the room fills with 30 or so in the hall.

In the court room are a jury of twelve men half of whom are soldiers, there is a police officer making notes, HANDLER and PAGE are at the back of the hall.

NEVILLE JONES is the coroner. He brings the room to order and speaks to the jury.

> NEVILLE JONES
> *County of Dorset – Eastern District. Inquest No 160.*
>
> *Gentlemen of the jury – I much regret the necessity for calling you together today to enquire into the circumstances leading up to the death of a very gallant Officer known at the time of his death as Thomas Edward Shaw, but better known to the world in general as Colonel Lawrence of Arabia.*

NEVILLE JONES (continuing)
Despite the skill and devotion of the eminent medical men who attended him and the Hospital Staff he died on Sunday last. When you have heard the evidence it will be for you to bring in your verdict. As to the actual cause of death you will have the evidence of Captain Allen, the Army Specialist who with Mr Cairns conducted a post mortem examination and therefore on this point your verdict will be in accordance with the medical evidence.

FADE TO the first witness, CAPTAIN CHARLES ALLEN

CAPT. CHARLES ALLEN
I am a Captain in the Royal Army Medical Corps. At about 11.45 a.m. on the 13th May 1935 the Deceased, Mr T. E. Shaw and Hargraves were both admitted to the Hospital at Bovington. I quickly examined Hargraves and found he was not seriously injured. At this time Mr Shaw was being carried up to the Theatre. I then examined Mr Shaw and found him deeply unconscious.

CAPT. CHARLES ALLEN (continuing)
I came to the conclusion he was suffering from severe head injuries. I had the skull x-rayed which showed a fracture. The Deceased remained unconscious until his death at 8 a.m. on the 19th May 1935. With consent of the relatives I made a post mortem examination in conjunction with Mr Cairns. We found a large fissured fracture 9 inches long extending from the left side of the head backwards to the middle line - across the back of the skull and forward to the right side. Also small fracture of the orbital plate.

Page 100 of 120

CAPT. CHARLES ALLEN (continuing)
*The brain was very severely lacerated especially
on the left side. Prior to death congestion of the
lungs had set in and heart failure. In my
opinion the cause of death was fracture of the
skull and laceration of the brain, heart failure
and congestion of the lungs.*

*In Mr Cairns and my opinions there were such
severe lacerations and damage to the brain that
in the event of his recovery he would have only
regained partial use of his speech and eyesight.
Had Mr Shaw lived he would have been unable
to speak and would have lost his memory and
would have been paralysed.*

Fade to:

The next witness, the other cyclist, FRANK FLETCHER.
He has been well rehearsed.

FRANK FLETCHER (as if being read))
*I live at 50 Elles Road, Bovington Camp, and I
am 14 years of age. On 13th May 1935 at about
11.20 a.m. I was riding a pedal bicycle from
Bovington Camp towards Clouds Hill and
Albert Hargraves was with me. I was riding in
front and Hargraves was riding at the back. I
was riding on the left of the road. When
opposite Clouds Hill Camp I heard a motorcycle coming up from behind. I then heard a
crash and Bert's bicycle fell on top of me and
knocked me off my bicycle.*

*I got up and saw Mr Lawrence go over the
handle bars of the motor-cycle and fall about 5
yards in front. I went to Bert who gave me his
butcher's book and I saw 3 pennies lying on the
road. He then seemed to fall asleep. I saw a lot of
men running over from the tents.*

NEVILLE JONES
Did you see any other vehicles on the road?

FRANK FLETCHER
No sir. There were no cars on the road then. I did not pass a car from the time I left Bovington Camp and the accident.

NEVILLE JONES
Did you leave the road at any time?

FRANK FLETCHER
We did not leave the road at all sir.

NEVILLE JONES
Were you riding in the middle of the road?

FRANK FLETCHER
I was riding close to the left-hand side — between one and two yards. When the crash occurred the other boy was not at my side. I do not know what part of the road the motor-cyclist was on at the time of the accident. After Bert's bicycle struck me I looked up and saw the motor-cycle about 5 yards in front in the direction in which I was going and the rider going over the handle bars. We had been riding one behind the other for about 100 yards.

Fade to:

The next witness, the other cyclist ALBERT HARGRAVES also well rehearsed. His head and arm are bandaged.

ALBERT HARGRAVES
I am 14 years of age and live at 56b Somme Road, Bovington Camp. I am employed as an errand boy by Dodge & Co, Butchers, Bovington Camp.

ALBERT HARGREAVES (continuing)
On 13th May 1935 I was cycling from Bovington Camp to Waddock Cross, Turners Puddle and Frank Fletcher was with me for company.

Opposite Clouds Hill Camp I was riding 4 or 5 feet behind Fletcher and on the left-hand side of the road. I heard the sound of a motor-cycle coming from behind. No motor car passed me about this time or any traffic of any sort. I do not remember any more until I found myself in Hospital. I do not even remember being thrown off my bicycle.

NEVILLE JONES
How were you riding your bicycles? Were you talking? How were you positioned on the road?

ALBERT HARGRAVES
When we left the camp we were riding abreast. We changed positions because of the noise of the motor-cycle. We had been riding in single file for about 80 yards and we were not talking and had been riding one behind the other for about 10 minutes. I slowed up and got behind Frank. I did not wobble at all. The road was not uneven at the side where I was riding. We were riding at a normal pace with both hands on the handlebars.

NEVILLE-JONES examines a photograph of the bicycles.

NEVILLE JONES
Given your stature the bicycle seems somewhat large for you?

ALBERT HARGRAVES
The bicycle is the right size for me but I have to reach a little for the pedals.

Fade to:

The next witness, the other cyclist CORPORAL ERNEST CATCHPOLE.

> ERNEST CATCHPOLE
> *I am Corporal No 7581979 Ernest Catchpole of the Royal Army Ordnance Corps, stationed at Tidworth. At about 11.20 a.m. on May 13th 1935 I was at Clouds Hill Camping Ground and about 100 yards from the road. I heard the noise of a motor-cycle coming from the direction of Bovington Camp.*
>
> *I saw the motor-cycle which was going between 50 and 60 miles an hour. Just before the motor-cycle got level with the Camp it passed a black car.*
>
> *It was a private car. The car was on its proper side of the road. I then saw the motor-cyclist swerve across the road to avoid two pedal cyclists going in the same direction. The motor-cyclist swerved immediately after he passed the car which was going in the opposite direction.*
>
> *I should say the collision occurred about 15 to 20 feet after the motor cyclist had passed the car.*
>
> *I then heard a crash and saw the motor-cycle twisting and turning over and over along the road. I immediately went to the road and called for help.*
>
> *I found the motor-cyclist lying on the right-hand side of the road — his face was covered in blood and I sent to the Camp for a stretcher.*

ERNEST CATCHPOLE (continuing)
An Army lorry came along and I asked them to take the injured persons to Hospital which they did. One of the pedal-cyclists was lying some distance down the road on the left side. I did not actually see the accident happen.

NEVILLE JONES
Were the cyclists riding single file or two abreast?

ERNEST CATCHPOLE (hesitates)
I do not know whether the pedal-cyclists were riding one behind the other or abreast. But there would have been sufficient room for the motor-cyclist to pass between the car and the pedal-cyclists if the motor-cyclist had not been going at such a speed.

HANDLER sitting next to PAGE at the back of the hall smiles. The whitewash sticks.

Fade to:

NEVILLE JONES summing up.

NEVILLE JONES
The only additional information concerns that of the motorcycle – a Brough Superior. We have a statement from the manufacturer, Mr George Brough. He says it was little damaged and on examination no obvious mechanical fault was apparent.

The only conflicting point in the evidence seems to be that with regard to the car. I do not necessarily mean that the car had anything to do with the accident but the fact that Corporal Catchpole is certain that he saw it and the boys are certain that they did not is rather unsatisfactory.

Page 105 of 120

NEVILLE JONES (continuing)
You have now heard the evidence and I do not think you will have any difficulty in arriving at your verdict. The facts are only too clear and that the collision was an accident there can be no doubt, what caused the Deceased to run into the pedal-cyclist from the rear we shall never know, but the evidence would lead one to think that Mr Shaw must have been travelling at a very fast speed and possibly lost control of his motorcycle.

I do not think there can be any other conclusion on the evidence. Under the circumstances you will doubtless consider the proper verdict to bring in will be one of accidental death.

Fade to:

NEVILLE JONES being handed a piece of paper by the Foreman of the Jury. He nods to the jury and opens the paper. He is in agreement with the verdict.

NEVILLE JONES
The verdict. Died from injuries received accidentally.

Needless to say, I entirely concur in your verdict. I am sure you would wish me to convey your sympathy as well as my own to Mr Shaw's relatives in the loss they and our country have sustained through the untimely death of such a gallant Englishman.

This inquest is therefore adjourned.

Fade to:

The court room emptying. PAGE stands in the court room doorway. HANDLER approaches NEVILLE JONES.

>   HANDLER
> *You will omit your statement regarding the black car I'm sure from your final records?*
>
>   NEVILLE JONES
> *Of course, of course. With the witnesses at variance I don't see any reason to set any hares running unnecessarily.*
>
>   HANDLER
> *Quite so. Quite so.*

HANDLER walks from the court room. He is the last in the room and closes the doors behind him.

Scene 31 – The Funeral			
Location	St Nicholas Church, Moreton	**Est. Run Time**	4:00
Synopsis Mr T.E. Shaw's funeral.			

Fade to:

Interior / ST NICHOLAS CHURCH MORETON / DAY

CAPTION: 21st May 1935 at 2pm

CAMERA POV from the pulpit shows the church full of mourners.

They include FLORENCE HARDY, ARTHUR RUSSELL, WINSTON CHURCHILL, LADY ASTOR, LORD LLOYD, SIEGFRIED SASSON, ROBERT GRAVES, Senior Officers from all the forces.

LAWRENCE'S coffin is draped in Union Flag on a small four-wheeled cart in front of the altar.

The congregation chant Psalm 121:

> CONGREGATION
> *I will lift up mine eyes unto the hills, from whence cometh my help.*
> *My help cometh from the Lord, which made heaven and earth.*

Fade to:

> *The Lord shall preserve thee from all evil: he shall preserve thy soul.*
> *The Lord shall preserve thy going out and thy coming in from this time forth, and even for evermore.*

Cut to:

INT / MORETON CHURCH   Day

CAMERA is from behind LORD LLOYD looking down on the congregation and who completes a litany to LAWRENCE from the pulpit.

> LORD LLOYD
> *He was one of those rare beings who seemed to belong to the morning of the world. His end would have pleased him.*
>
> *A swift rush and a silent passing.*

The congregation sing hymn "Jesu Lover of My Soul" to the tune ABERYSTWYTH.

> CONGREGATION
> *Jesus, lover of my soul, let me to Thy bosom fly,*
> *While the nearer waters roll, while the tempest still is high.*
> *Hide me, O my Saviour, hide, till the storm of life is past;*
> *Safe into the haven guide; O receive my soul at last.*
> *Other refuge have I none, hangs my helpless soul on Thee;*
> *Leave, ah! leave me not alone, still support and comfort me.*
> *All my trust on Thee is stayed, all my help from Thee I bring;*
> *Cover my defenceless head with the shadow of Thy wing.*

FADE OUT hymn singing; FADE IN grand orchestral and instrumental version of ABERYSTWYTH

Fade to:

INT / MORETON CHURCH   Day

The pall bearers – ARTHUR RUSSELL, ERIC KENNINGTON, PAT KNOWLES, COLONEL NEWCOMBE, SIR RONALD STORRS, AIRCRAFTMAN W. BRADBURY move the coffin through the church.

Cut to:

Exterior / MORETON COUNTRY LANE   Day

Note for Reference – Pathe News Reel of Lawrence's Funeral.

The lane is lined with mourners as the pall bearers move the carriage down the lane to the churchyard. Behind the coffin the mourners are led by CHURCHILL, LADY ASTOR, LORD LLOYD and other dignitaries.

Cut to:

Exterior / MORETON CEMETERY   Day

Coffin is laid on its supports over the grave. As it is laid in the ground the grass from Aqaba is laid upon its lid. It is lowered into the ground.

The cemetery is packed, not only with mourners but "tourists" and reporters.

The mourners gradually leave the graveside. CHURCHILL, LADY ASTOR, LORD LLOYD leave through the gates.

> LADY ASTOR
> *Lawrence was tremendously outspoken. He was direct and sometimes brutally honest. Do you know he described me as tiring and wild mare in his last letter to me?*
>
> Commentin.

> WINSTON CHURCHILL (wryly)
> *Indeed? He was certainly honest. .* A man of rare decency?

They continue to walk a few yards from the cemetery and view the clamour. CHURCHILL turns to LADY ASTOR and LORD LLOYD.

> WINSTON CHURCHILL (angrily)
> *This is not England's proudest moment. We have lost a great man. I fear whatever our need in the coming years we shall never see his like again.*

At the graveside a reporter tries to take a photograph of the grave. ARTHUR RUSSELL knocks the camera from his hand.

> ARTHUR RUSSELL
> *God may forgive you. Damn you! I don't!*

As the cemetery empties CAMERA focuses on FLORENCE HARDY who is now alone in the cemetery. She places a wreath at the graveside. The card reads: "To TEL who should sleep with Kings".

TIME LAPSE photograph shows the grave filled and covered with flowers, bluebells, campions, buttercups, forget-me-nots, rhododendrons, lilacs.

Time passes.

TIME LAPSE then shows the grave cleared with just a rough hewn cross.

Time passes

TIME LAPSE then shows the grave with its current gravestone.

Scene 32 – Catchpole's Suicide

Location	Western Desert, Egypt	Est. Run Time	1:30

Synopsis
Catchpole's suicide.

Dissolve to:

Exterior / WESTERN DESERT, EGYPT   Night

CAPTION: July 1940, Egypt Western Desert

CAMERA shows SERGEANT ERNEST CATCHPOLE dressed in desert shirt and shorts in a deckchair.

CATCHPOLE looks up at a crescent desert moon and the starlight. It is a beautiful night.

By hurricane lamp he looks at a photo of his wife and daughter and reads a recent letter from his wife. On the table is a copy of the "Seven Pillars of Wisdom" by T.E. LAWRENCE and he places a hand upon it as if it is his Bible. In his head he hears LAWRENCE'S voice:

> T.E. LAWRENCE V/O
> *This creed of the desert seemed inexpressible in words, and indeed in thought.*

CATCHPOLE smiles, stands and walks back to the tent with the letter, photographs and picks up his service revolver.

Cut to:

Interior / ARMY HUT IN THE DESERT   Night

CATCHPOLE climbs in the top bunk and polishes the revolver.

Cut to:

Exterior / DESERT NIGHT SKY   Night

There is an ominous "bang" of a single pistol shot.

Cut to:

Interior / SMALL ARMY HUT IN THE DESERT   Day

CATCHPOLE is dead on the top bunk, his eyes stare blankly. The gun lies smoking on the floor. Blood oozes from a single bullet hole in CATCHPOLE'S forehead.

Scene 33 – End Titles and Credits			
Location	Moreton Cemetery	**Est. Run Time**	2:30

Synopsis
Epilogue.

Cut to:

Exterior / MORETON CEMETERY   Day

CAMERA shows T.E. LAWRENCE'S grave stone in the present day. A single rose sits on the grave.

CAMERA PANS to beautiful blue sky on an English summer's day. The sounds of gently rustling trees and skylarks fill the air.

> T.E. LAWRENCE V/O
> *I loved you, so I drew these tides of men into my hands and wrote my will across the sky in stars. To gain you Freedom, the seven-pillared worthy house, that your eyes might be shining for me, when I came.*

Dissolve to:

NEWREEL - WW2 Footage including Churchill.

1938	German unites with Austria. Occupies Sudetenland
1939	Germany invade Poland; WW2 starts
1940	The Nazis occupy Denmark, Norway, Holland, Belgium and France.
1941	Germany attacks Russia; USA enters the war
1944	Normandy Landings
1945	Allies enter Germany. Hitler commits suicide
1945	War in Europe ends. VE Day Celebrations.

CAPTION: *Churchill stated that it was the work of British Secret Service which shortened the conflict by more than two years. Furthermore he told King George VI: "It was thanks to this intelligence that we won the war."*

CAPTION: *Postscript: Sir Hugh Cairns who conducted Lawrence's post-mortem pioneered legislation for protective headgear by motorcyclists. Over subsequent decades, this has saved countless lives.*

FADE TO BLACK.

Fade to:

CREDITS ROLE

MUSIC – Beethoven Piano Sonata No. 8 Adagio Cantabile

MUSIC – Beethoven Symphony No. 7 in A Major Op 02 II Allegretto.

CREDITS should include a rolling montage of photographs, in chronological order from LAWRENCE'S life from the earliest days to the final photograph taken with his motorbike.

END CLOSING CREDITS

FADE TO BLACK.

THE END

Biographies

T.E. Lawrence (aka T.E. Shaw)

Lieutenant Colonel Thomas Edward Lawrence, CB, DSO (16 August 1888 – 19 May 1935), known as T. E. Lawrence, was a British Army officer renowned especially for his liaison role during the Arab Revolt against Turkish rule of 1916–18. It was during this period that he found friendship – some say a homosexual one - with an Arab boy Selim Ahmed nicknamed **Dahoum** - 'little dark one'.

The extraordinary breadth and variety of his activities and associations, and his ability to describe them vividly in writing, earned him international fame as Lawrence of Arabia. Lawrence's public image was due in part to American journalist Lowell Thomas' sensationalised reporting of the revolt as well as to Lawrence's autobiographical account "Seven Pillars of Wisdom" published in 1922.

Winston Churchill

Sir Winston Leonard Spencer-Churchill, KG, OM, CH, TD, PC, DL, FRS, Hon. RA (30 November 1874 – 24 January 1965) was a British statesman known for his leadership of the United Kingdom during the Second World War. He is widely regarded as one of the great wartime leaders and served as Prime Minister twice (1940–45 and 1951–55).

He met Lawrence in 1921 when Lawrence is invited to join Churchill's Colonial Office as an Adviser on Arab Affairs. Lawrence and Churchill would stay in contact until Lawrence's death in 1935.

Thomas Hardy

Thomas Hardy, OM (2 June 1840 – 11 January 1928) was an English novelist and poet. While he regarded himself primarily as a poet who composed novels mainly for financial gain, he became and continues to be widely regarded for his novels such as Tess of the d'Urbervilles and Far from the Madding Crowd. The bulk of his fictional works, initially published as serials in magazines, were set in the semi-fictional land of Wessex (based on the Dorchester region where he grew up) and explored tragic characters struggling against their passions and social circumstances.

First meets Lawrence in May 1923 when Lawrence settled at Cloud's Hill a short distance from Hardy's home near Dorchester.

Major-Gen. Sir Vernon George Kell, KBE

(21 November 1873 – 27 March 1942) Founder and first Director General of the British Security Service, otherwise known as MI5.

During World War I, Kell headed the MI5 section dealing with the Indian seditionist movement in Europe, called MI5. Among Kell's officers worked ex-ICS officers Robert Nathan and H.L Stephenson.

In May 1940 Kell was removed from office by Winston Churchill, he was knighted for his services shortly before his death in 1942. While Director General of the British Security Service he was known as 'K'

E. M. Forster

Edward Morgan Forster was born in London on the first day of 1879. Forster became a writer shortly after graduating from King's College. His first novels were products of that particular time -- stories about the changing social conditions during the decline of Victorianism. He developed this theme in his first novels, Where Angels Fear to Tread (1905) and The Longest Journey (1907), followed by the comic novel A Room With a View (1908). Forster's first major success was Howard's End (1910).

Forster spent three wartime years in Alexandria doing civilian work and visited India twice. After he returned to England, inspired by his experience, he wrote A Passage to India (1924). A Passage to India is the last novel Forster published during his lifetime. Maurice was written circa 1914, but published in 1971 after Forster's death. Forster specifically requested the novel be published only after his death due to its overt homosexual theme.

Henry Williamson

Known as the Dreamer of Devon he is mainly known as the author of Tarka the Otter, a book praised by Thomas Hardy, Galsworthy, TE Lawrence and many others, and which won for him the prestigious Hawthornden Prize 1928. A controversial and eccentric man, actually encompassed an enormously wide range of writing from his life's experiences soldier, writer, broadcaster, naturalist, farmer and writer. Active in the British Fascist Movement.

Photographs

Frank Fletcher

Thomas Hardy

Florence Hardy

Dahoum

Sharif Ali

Lord Lloyd

George Brough

Sydney Smith

Lady Astor

Eric Kennington

Gin

Sealyham Terrier

No photographs were found for Albert Hargraves, Ernest Catchpole, Neville-Jones, Peter Page, John Prentice, Douglas Cake. Captain Charles Allen, Arthur Russell, E "Posh" Palmer. John Handler and Captain Hyde-Pierce are fictional characters.

About The Author

Mark J.T. Griffin

(comes from lots of different places but this time around) was born in March 1958 in Wolverhampton.

He lives in Warwickshire with his wife Ingrid, daughters Dani & Steph, Sam and Lily the Labradors and cats Bramble & Bracken.

He divides his spare time between writing, music, drama, theatre and re-enacting Civil War battles. Since the mid-eighties he has written numerous articles and short stories on subjects ranging from clocks to computers to Custer.

In 1994 he wrote the acclaimed biography, **Vangelis: The Unknown Man** and in 1997 the new-age adventure novel *going home*.

This was following in 2006 by the novel *Richard of Eastwell* based on his love of history and theatre. The Cathar Prophecy, his third novel followed in 2007. His most recent novel **ANGEL HOUSE** was published in early in 2011.